SANCTUARY

Sanctuary
Copyright © 2024 by Ilona Andrews
EBOOK ISBN: 9781641972864
KDP POD ISBN: 9798327674332
IS POD ISBN: 9781641972918

NYLA Publishing
121 W. 27th St, Suite 1201, NY 10001, New York.
http://www.nyliterary.com

SANCTUARY

ROMAN'S CHRONICLES
BOOK 1

ILONA ANDREWS

LETTER TO THE READER

S lavic mythology is Roman's bread and butter. His is a magical world, filled with creatures and gods that were once worshipped and feared by the many Slavic tribes of Eastern Europe. Unfortunately, due to the absence of written records from historic practitioners, most of what we know about Slavic mythology comes to us via oral traditions or accounts of foreign historians. This is a work of fiction, presenting our own, fantasy version of Slavic mythology as it exists in the Kate Daniels series. We took liberties with the source material in the name of artistic license. This story isn't an academic paper and shouldn't be used as such.

To help you make sense of it, we've included a brief overview of some Slavic folklore in the extras, a glossary of mythological terms, and a list of the gods and monsters.

Thank you to Shayera Tangri for her help with pronunciations of the Zoroastrian terms.

[1]

S now crunched under his feet. It spread in front of him like a glittering blanket, a foot deep, sheathing the vast plain he was crossing, and he sank a little with every step. Above, a night sky gaped like a hole in existence, a spray of stars floating in its black depths.

He didn't know how long he had been walking. It felt like forever. He didn't know his destination either. He only felt it, pulling him like a magnet toward the dark wall of colossal pines at the edge of the plain.

Step. Another step.

Bitter cold bit at his face. His nose had gone numb, and he could barely feel his fingers in his thick red mittens as he clutched the rope that was pulled tight over his shoulder.

He was holding a rope. Why?

It felt strange somehow.

He stopped and looked over his shoulder. An enormous fir tree lay on the snow behind him. The rope was wrapped around its trunk. Behind it, a long trail of rough snow marked his wake and rolled off into the horizon. He had dragged the tree for miles.

The field around him tore like a paper screen.

Roman opened his eyes and stared at the ceiling of his

bedroom. His back ached. Things snapped into focus. The tree, the harness, the destination, everything made sense.

Fucking hell.

He sat up slowly, fighting soreness. His whole body protested, whining against the movement. Tomorrow was December twenty-fourth. The thought turned his stomach.

Being the priest of a dark god came with certain obligations. Obligations he honored with dedication and discipline. But a man had his limits. This was his. His god knew it. Roman was available any other time of the year, but from December twenty-third to December twenty-fifth he was to be left alone. Such was their unspoken agreement for the last seven years.

Roman didn't expect kindness. Chernobog was the God of Destruction, Darkness, and Death, the Black Flame, the Final Cold, the End of Everything. Hoping for kindness would be foolish, and he wasn't a foolish man. No, he had expected fairness. Chernobog, for all his many faults and temper tantrums, was unfailingly fair.

Roman stared at the rumpled covers. He had this vague but disturbing anxiety, as if he'd either forgotten to do something important or something vital had gone missing and he couldn't figure out what. It irritated him to no end.

The foul mood was nothing new. He detested the end of December. Koliada, Christmas, Saturnalia, he hated every iteration of the Winter Rites, with all of their corresponding rituals. The entire season was a wash. He didn't decorate, he tried his damnedest not to celebrate, and the only thing he did like about it was the food.

Roman threw the covers aside, wincing against the cold air. Naked as a newborn. Ugh. His crumpled pajama pants lay on the floor. He must've stripped in his sleep, because why the hell not? It's not like it was the middle of winter and his house felt like an icebox.

He growled under his breath, got up, picked up his clothes—

predictably soaked in sweat—and headed to the bathroom. He tossed them into the hamper, relieved himself, and went to brush his teeth. A big red welt crossed his chest, a souvenir from the rope. Great. Just great.

His reflection was looking leaner, too. Years ago, as he'd trudged through the wilderness half-starved, with a hundred extra pounds of gear on his back, next to other young fools in the same pixelated Army camo, he promised himself that when he got out, he would eat more and move less. Old, fat, and happy. That was the goal.

He was thirty-four years old now, and if he skipped a few meals, the flesh melted off him, leaving behind muscle and gristle, as if being in service to Chernobog burned him from the inside out. If he wasn't careful, he'd end up like his father, a gaunt old man with a perpetual frown stuck on his face.

He put on sweatpants, a T-shirt, and an old sweatshirt so soft and worn, it was threadbare. It felt familiar, and right now familiar was good.

It was a bad idea for him to be alone around this time. He'd planned on spending the holiday with Ashley, a lawyer with long legs and a fondness for light spanking, but Ashley was no longer around. He couldn't really blame her. Sooner or later, they all ran.

His only other option was family. The thought made Roman shudder. They would be celebrating Koliada, the Winter Festival. The entire clan would be at his uncle's house right now, getting ready for the monster parade and putting the finishing touches on the tree. The tree had been borrowed from the Christians, who in turn stole it from other pagans, but nobody cared anymore where it came from. Tomorrow night a noisy, happy crowd of Slavic neopagans would pummel each other in the ritual brawl, sing songs, then eat, get roaring drunk, and exchange gifts, while he sat there like a dark icicle, alone, wrapped in a swirl of human warmth but untouched by it.

Family would only make it worse. He would have to make an

appearance tomorrow, and he would need to look upbeat and unbothered, because if he let what he was feeling show on his face, they would smother him trying to make him feel better. He didn't want the attention. He didn't want to think about it or talk about it. No, he had to look like he had his shit together, and that meant taking care of himself now and covering his bases. He'd build a fire to get warm, make some coffee, eat some good food, and sink into a book to live in someone else's head for a change. He still had eggnog in the fridge and the cookies he'd baked two nights ago.

Gods, eggnog sounded good right now.

Roman shoved his feet into the Eeyore slippers his eldest sister had bought him last year and headed into the living room. He'd gone to sleep with a well-stocked fire that should've lasted until morning. Instead, a pile of ashes greeted him. If he were lucky, there would be some coals under all that.

Had he been born several decades ago, he would've just turned on the central heating. He'd have lived in a subdivision, his lawn ornaments would have been ceramic gnomes or cute animals, and he'd have had a comfortable, prosaic job, something like an insurance adjuster. But the world had suffered a magic apocalypse. Now magic waves battered the planet, coming and going as they pleased, leaving the skyscrapers in ruins, and continuing his family business meant a lifetime of servitude as the priest of a dark god...

He caught himself. That way lay dragons, and not the fun kind. He needed eggnog. Eggnog would make everything better.

Roman went into the kitchen. The long window above the sink presented him with a dreary view: a chunk of gray sky above a stretch of lawn, dusted with snow and edged by dark woods. His kingdom in all of its glory.

There would be more snow before spring. The magic waves had been getting stronger lately, and this year they brought unseasonable cold. The temperature had dropped into the mid-twenties last week and stayed there. Even during the mildest Atlanta winters, his house always got a little snow—it came with the territory. But now, with the frigid temperatures, a snowpocalypse was almost guaranteed. He had no doubt about it.

Eggnog and cookies, and then he would brave the outside and bring more wood in.

Roman swung the fridge door open. An empty jug of eggnog greeted him. He was sure it had been half-full yesterday. Did he drink it all and forget? He stared at it for a hot minute, but the jug refused to refill itself.

Fine. He would have coffee with his cookies.

He shut the fridge and turned to the island. Last night he'd left a plate of cookies on it under a glass hood. The hood was still there. So was the plate. The cookies were gone. Only crumbs remained.

"What the actual fuck?"

The house didn't answer.

He lifted the hood and stared at the crumbs. A little sparkle caught his eye. He leaned closer.

Glitter. A little smudge of silver glitter on the rim of the plate.

Magic gave thoughts power. Faith was a form of thought, so if a group of people believed in a specific being with all their heart, it could manifest into existence. The more believers there were, the higher the chances of manifestation, and the more power the being would have. Faith endowed the Pope with his miraculous healing powers and spawned region-specific monsters based on urban legends and folklore.

However, sometimes the very nature of the imagined being precluded the manifestation from occurring because fulfilling it would require infinite power. For example, it didn't matter how many people believed that a white-bearded man in a jolly red suit delivered presents on Christmas. For that manifestation to occur, a single being would have to be aware of every single child, assess their conduct throughout an entire year, create a toy out of thin air, and then deliver it simultaneously to every household with a child. The scale was too large, and the very faith that kept the legend alive ensured it would never become reality.

This was his bread and butter. His father and uncle, in a rare feat of cooperation, had literally written a book on it and called it *The Santa Claus Paradox*.

The chance that Santa Claus had manifested in his kitchen and stolen his cookies was absolutely zero. Besides, it wasn't even Christmas Eve.

Roman tilted his head to the side. A second sprinkling of glitter sparkled at him from the edge of the island. This one had a dark brown smudge near it.

He skirted the island and studied the smudge. Blood. Roman passed his hand over it. Magic nipped at his skin. Human.

A human covered in glitter had crossed the minefield of magic defenses surrounding his house, broken in without tripping any of the alarms, drank his eggnog, ate his cookies, bled on his kitchen island, and then disappeared.

Honestly, Santa Claus was more likely.

Roman squinted at the smudge and bent down, putting himself on the same level as it. Another sparkle of glitter, on the other counter. A little swipe across the gas stove, a shiny trace across the counter, and a small, shiny pawprint on the left pane of the window. The locks on the window had been disengaged.

Damn it.

He growled, stomped through the house to the back door, yanked it open, and strode out onto the back porch. It was bitterly cold. A thin layer of snow covered the lawn. He had thought it was morning, but it had to be late afternoon judging by the shadows. He must've lost time dragging that damn tree across the field.

Roman scanned the grounds.

Thirty yards away, a pack of small, creepy creatures crowded a tall fir tree, decorated with random ornaments, pieces of tin foil, pinecones, red berries, moss, feathers, and assorted forest trash.

Roman's left eye twitched. For a second, he simply stared.

Slavic pagan tradition was filled with small nasties, traditionally seen as evil or, at the very least, a nuisance. Little critters that ranged from annoying to sinister. According to the folklore, they stared from the darkness with glowing eyes, made weird scuttling noises on the roof, stole things, spooked the livestock and scared the children, spread trash when it was swept into a pile, bit people's ankles, served as sorcerers' minions, and generally created havoc. Collectively known as nechist—"unclean things"—they loved him with undying devotion. He'd given up on shooing them ages ago and now fed them kitchen scraps and chicken feed.

All of the usual suspects were here. His tame anchutka—covered in squirrel fur, with the body of a lemur, the tail of a possum, leathery wings, and the face of a nightmarish bush baby—stood on her hind legs, trying to hang a big red ball on a branch. The melalo, a plump two-headed bird, with one head dead and drooping to the side, clutched a bright blue feather in his beak and kept shoving it at the anchutka.

An assortment of kolovershi, ranging in size from a cardinal to a barn owl, flitted from branch to branch, tucking things in. Furry, with long ears that stood straight up, scaly limbs, and dexterous paws armed with small but sharp talons, they looked like some mutated versions of the Furby toys he remembered from his childhood, equipped with shining eyes and fuzzy wings. They had just shown up on his porch one night. Kolovershi served witches, and these were clearly orphaned, so he had taken them to his mother. She'd tried to place them with other witches, but they just kept coming back.

The auka, a Russian hamster-looking mouse the size of a possum with tan fur, tiny antlers, and a skunk's fluffy tan tail, dashed through the branches, trying to wrap a long glittering garland around the tree. Kor, the one pet nechist he did not mind, was holding the garland up in his cat paws. A korgorusha, he resembled a black cat with an abnormally long, prehensile tail and trailed smoke wherever he went.

And finally Roro. Nobody knew what the fuck Roro was. She was fourteen inches tall, weighed about twenty-five pounds and stood on four sturdy legs armed with sharp, retractable claws. Her squished face looked almost cute in an ugly but adorable way, but her wide mouth was filled with razor-sharp fangs, and her body with its bunny tail was solid muscle. When she got going, she was like a bowling ball, wrecking everything in her path. Currently, she was dashing back and forth around the tree for no apparent reason. Reason, in general, wasn't Roro's strong suit.

As he watched, Roro hopped over something sticking out from behind the tree. A leg. A human leg in a boot.

Roman sucked in a deep breath. "What the fuck do you think you're doing?"

The motley crew froze. The anchutka dropped the ball in the snow. Kor vanished in a puff of dark smoke. Roro slid to a stop and backed away, tall, fluffy ears flat against her head. The auka raised a small hand-paw and waved.

He marched off the porch toward the tree. The kolovershi squeaked and hid in the fir branches. The anchutka scuttled aside.

"What the hell is going on here?"

The melalo looked left, looked right, not sure what the best route to escape was, and then stared at him, terrified. Roman gave him a look.

"How many times do I have to tell you, you're a Romani demon. Go be with your people!"

The melalo squawked and ran across the snow, diving under the tree.

"And you!"

The auka blinked.

"You're not even a nechist. You're a forest spirit. Why are you here? Why are any of you here?"

The auka waved at him again.

"At least have the decency to act contrite."

He finally rounded the tree. An unconscious teenager hugged the trunk, curled into a fetal ball. Judging by the dusting of snow on his jacket, he had been there a while. A dark red stain spread over his jeans—something had either bitten or stabbed his thigh. Someone had stuck a Christmas wreath, no doubt stolen off some door, onto his head and shoved a little artificial Christmas twig with glitter and bright plastic berries into his exposed left ear. Tinsel wrapped his jacket, binding him to the tree. A small chunk of cookie stuck out from between his lips, smudged with glitter.

"Where did you get this human?"

Nobody answered.

He slapped his hand over his twitching eye, pulled the shiny twig out of the boy's ear, plucked the cookie out of his mouth, tossed the wreath aside, grabbed him by the shoulder, and shook him.

"Hey kid?"

The boy's eyelashes fluttered. He uncurled a little and Roman glimpsed a small black puppy in the curve of his body.

"You can't stay here," Roman told him. "It's dangerous for you here."

The kid's lips moved. A little blood dripped onto his chin. He struggled to say something.

Roman crouched by him.

"Sanctuary," the kid whispered.

"What?"

"Sanctuary..."

"Where do you think you are? Does this look like a Christian church to you? Do you see a priest's collar on my neck?"

The kid's eyes rolled back into his head, and he went limp.

Damn it.

Logs crackled in the fire, sending an occasional burst of orange sparks into the air. Warmth permeated the house.

Roman set the squirt bottle with saline aside and gulped his coffee. It was bitter and hot. He'd gotten used to drinking it black while in the service, because cream and sugar had been scarce, and he'd never lost the habit.

The kid lay on a pad of blankets in front of the fireplace with a towel under his injured leg. Roman had cut his jeans to expose the wound, and the laceration glistened with red, like an angry mouth. Something had slashed the kid's thigh, cutting a four-inch gap through the muscle. A pretty deep cut, too. A couple of inches to the left, and he would've bled out. His face wasn't too bad. Someone had punched him in the mouth, but all of his teeth were still there.

Roman slipped latex gloves on—worth their weight in gold, literally, since rubber was pricy post-Shift—pulled the suture needle from its boiling water bath with needle drivers and set about threading it.

The kid looked about fifteen, dark hair, pale skin, about five foot ten or so. Slight build. Not from starvation, but from that typical thinness adolescents get when they grow six inches in one summer. He hadn't had enough time to fill out.

His clothes said someone took good care of him. His jeans didn't show much wear, his sweatshirt was relatively clean, and he wore Mahrous boots. Most boots were now custom-made by small shops, but in Atlanta, Mahrous Bootmakers stood above the rest. A good pair of their boots would last years, and they came with a hefty price tag. Only a loving parent would invest that much money in something an adolescent might outgrow in a few months.

All in all, nothing stood out. Just your regular, typical kid, probably from a better part of the city. Didn't look familiar.

The little black puppy curled tightly against the boy's body, looking like an oversized doughnut of black fur. The puppy was female, probably a black German Shepherd, and checking her over didn't reveal any obvious injuries. As soon as he'd set the puppy back down, she'd scrambled back to the boy and huddled against him.

Smoke swirled on the couch and congealed into Kor. The korgorusha twitched his long, tufted ears, and shifted his weight, resting his big body on his favorite blue pillow. His golden eyes shone with a soft light, half-magic, half-glow borrowed from the fire.

"Are we about to have visitors?"

The korgorusha purred. Vicious claws slid out of his soft black paws, pierced the pillow, and withdrew.

Figured.

Roman pulled the edges of the wound closed and made his first stitch. He'd have to wait until the rest of his misfit squad made it in for a detailed report.

At least the cut was nice and even. No ragged edges to trim.

The kid hadn't asked for shelter. He hadn't said, "Help!" or "I'm hurt." No, he'd said, "Sanctuary." That meant two things. First, the kid knew who Roman was and what he did for a living, and second, he was being chased.

Roman rolled his wrist, taking care to pierce the skin carefully. The fact that he didn't recognize the kid meant nothing. There were roughly 10,000 Slavic neopagans in Atlanta and four times that number of other pagan religion practitioners, and that wasn't counting people of Slavic descent and their friends and relatives who didn't actively worship but would look for magic solutions when trouble came clawing at their door. He couldn't possibly know everyone.

However, the fact that the kid showed up at his house at all was odd. Roman lived on fifteen acres in the woods, and the driveway to his property was a quarter of a mile long. His nearest neighbor was about half a mile away, a druid who wanted to nurture birds in solitude.

Very few people knew where he lived or how to get to his house. Most of the time petitioners came looking for his father or his uncle, sometimes his mother or sisters, and got passed down the chain to him. He was the last resort, called in either when everything else had failed or when things had gone so wrong from the start that nobody else wanted to touch the problem with a ten-foot pole.

How did the kid know where to find him? How did he get here? He'd had the nechist search the property, and they hadn't found a vehicle, a bicycle, or a horse. They didn't find a backpack or any bags and the boy didn't have a wallet either.

Last night the tech had been up, and Roman had walked the inner perimeter of his wards the same as he always did before he went to bed. Which meant the kid had entered the property sometime after Roman had gone to bed, but before the magic hit. The boy had run through the woods, bleeding all over, with nothing except his dog and the clothes on his back. The tree where he'd collapsed was only thirty yards from the house. The boy had to have seen the house but hadn't managed to get to it, which meant he'd been at his limit. The tree was as far as his body could go.

The cookie in his mouth came from a helpful kolovershi, who'd snuck into the house, depositing glitter and the boy's blood everywhere, ate the cookies, and then took one to the human child, because humans liked cookies and it would surely make him feel better. The culprit was probably Fedya, the smallest one of the flock. It seemed like a Fedya thing to do.

All of that added up to desperation.

Roman frowned. Two months ago, a family had come to his father begging and crying that their fourteen-year-old daughter had disappeared, and they were sure some unclean monstrosity had carried their Masha off because there was blood in her bedroom, a broken window, and claw marks on her windowsill. Roman had taken that mess on as a favor, and he'd found the kid in two hours at a trap house. She'd had a severe drug habit and an older boyfriend the family disapproved of, so she'd faked the whole thing so her parents would think she was dead and wouldn't look for her.

The boy on his blankets could be a runaway. In that case, he didn't want to get involved. He could barely resolve his own family disputes, let alone someone else's. Before he'd known about that fourteen-year-old, he would've said that a long trek across the woods while wounded was too drastic for a runaway. But Masha had run two miles in the freezing rain, wearing only her nightgown and slippers, before her scumbag boyfriend had picked her up—and she'd done it in the middle of the night during a magic wave, when anyone with a crumb of common sense would have stayed behind sturdy doors and solid walls. Teenagers thought they were immortal, and they could be both remarkably naïve and single-minded.

In the kitchen a window creaked, swinging open. The pack of kolovershi slipped into the room, arranged themselves on the floor in a ragged semicircle around him and the fire, and stared at him with glowing eyes.

He finished the last stitch, snipped the suture thread, set his tools down, and wrapped a fresh bandage over the wound. The kid didn't even stir. Roman checked his forehead. No fever. No cold sweat. He tossed a blanket over him and the puppy and peeled off his gloves.

"Let's see it."

The kolovershi flittered to him, dropping things into his palm: a chunk of bloody snow, weird metal-looking hairs, some dirt, some thread, and a clump of chewed-up tobacco dip. Ugh. The glamor of the job. So much glamor.

Roman tossed the lot into the fire and spat into the flames, sending a punch of magic through the logs. The fire turned a translucent, cold blue. Within it, twelve people trudged through the snowy forest, making their way up the old, half-overgrown road. At the front, a short, beefy guy gripped the leads of two oversized dogs. They stood about thirty-five inches at the shoulder, barrel-chested, front-heavy, like overbred pit bulls, and covered with odd bluish fur. A row of metallic spikes ran along their spines. Both dogs had their noses to the ground. Trackers out of the Honeycomb.

Nothing good ever came out of the Honeycomb.

He studied the procession. The two guys in front—the dog handler and a thinner man with lime-green hair who stuck close to him—had to be hired hands. Their clothes were shoddier. The ten people behind them were a different story. They wore gray Three Season duty jackets, matching gray pants tucked into boots, winter caps, and assault vests. Three had chest rigs with deep pockets, fully loaded. Probably magic users of some kind. All of them carried a crossbow and a rifle.

They didn't seem nervous. They weren't in a hurry. They moved methodically through the snow, following the dogs.

Ten professionals and two trackers. Overkill for a runaway kid.

The group passed a tall hickory, singed on one side. It had gotten struck by lightning three years ago, but magic had kept it alive. Unless the kid's trail led them in circles, they would reach the house in fifteen minutes.

Roman ended the spell, got up, washed his hands, and dried them with a kitchen towel. The little nasties watched him, ready to spring into action.

He went to the bedroom. The kolovershi followed him, sneaking in, peeking at him from around the corners. He entered his walk-in closet and opened a narrow cabinet. A six-foot tall staff waited inside, topped by the carved head of a monster bird.

Roman reached for it. His fingers touched the beech wood, polished and smooth. Magic nipped him. The bird's beak opened, and Klyuv let out a piercing screech.

The kolovershi froze.

"Shhh," Roman told it. "Not yet."

Klyuv clicked its beak, its cruel bird eyes turning in their orbits and fell silent.

Roman went to the front door and swung it open. The snow was inches deep now. The world had turned black and white—black trees on white snow, and against that monochromatic backdrop, the nechists' Christmas tree with its red and silver ornaments stood out like a challenge. Three sets of tracks led under it.

"Come here," Roman ordered.

The anchutka, the melalo, and Roro slipped out from under the tree and ran over to the porch. Roro bounded up the steps, stood up on her hind legs, and clawed at his pants. Her mouth opened. "*Roro.*"

"Sit."

Roro's butt landed on the floorboards.

The anchutka leaped, flew a little, and landed on Roman's shoulder. The melalo scooted by him, waddling anxiously from foot to foot. That was all of them. The kolovershi were already inside, and the auka had retreated to Chernobog's kumir in the backyard. Chernobog's idol, it was carved from a sacred beech tree, standing ten feet tall, and the auka had dug a long network of burrows beneath it. She would be safe there.

Roman raised his staff.

A bottomless darkness opened inside of him, a void churning with power and ice, straining to flow into him like a shadowy flood spilling into an empty vessel. He reached for it, grasped a thin current, and fed it into his staff.

Klyuv's beak gaped.

Roman brought the staff down, striking a sound from the porch boards. Magic the color of soot pulsed from the shaft, rushing through his property like a blast wave.

He owned fifteen acres, and two of them formed his backyard. The thorn fence that encircled it awoke, the branches sliding against each other. Ice daggers formed over the thorns.

Deep within the ground, under the frozen layer of topsoil, bones stirred.

The stop sign in the front yard shook, flinging snow off itself. The old, brown blood on it turned viscous. The words *KEEP OUT*, scrawled in a jagged script, bled anew. The Striga skull on top of the sign opened its thick jaw, snapping inhuman fangs. The runes carved in its forehead turned bright blue, and twin blue flames ignited in its empty orbits.

Roman surveyed the front yard. He'd rolled the unwelcome mat out. Now all he had to do was wait.

[2]

The child-hunters came out of the woods right on schedule.

Roman had parked himself on a chair in his living room, by the massive tinted front window and had a bit of his coffee. The front yard sloped slightly from the house, and this spot gave him a beautiful view of the entire battlefield. The nechist promptly arranged themselves around him, with Kor flopping himself on his lap.

They didn't have to wait long. First, a scout snuck up the driveway to view the house. He crouched by some snow-fluffed bushes, stared at the Striga skull for a bit, then retreated, and a few moments later two assholes circled the property in opposite directions and went to ground, one on the northeastern side and the other on the southwestern. They set up crossbows for the intersecting fields of fire and went still. Roman sent a couple of kolovershi to keep an eye on them.

Finally, the main force came up the driveway in a modified diamond formation: the two Honeycomb dickheads in the lead, armed with a dog each, followed by a pair of professionals; then the leader sandwiched between two more guys; another pair, and a rear guard.

"Someone was a good boy and read his manual on small unit tactics," Roman murmured.

This wasn't the way he would've gone about the raid, but he had a feeling they'd decided to bet on intimidation and surprise. One moment the woods were empty, the next there was a trained, well-armed squad taking position by the house. It would give most people pause.

He wasn't most people.

Roman put a pair of binoculars to his eyes.

The leader was tall and light-skinned, with a square jaw, short nose, and grayish stubble on his chin. Thick neck, some roundness in the face—well-fed. He hadn't been taking any long treks through the deep wilderness with a fifty-pound rucksack, eating MREs and pinecones recently. This was a mercenary, successful but gone a bit soft.

The leader squinted at the Striga skull on top of the stop sign, looking smug and slightly bored. The rest of his crew looked about the same—too much time at the gym, too much love for tactical sunglasses, too secure in their badassery. Active duty in the line of fire made people mean, lean, and half-feral, like starved wolves. These weren't wolves. They were guard dogs. Every single one of those guys knew where their next meal was coming from and where they would be sleeping that night.

Roman could practically hear what they were thinking. *This is overkill. We are better than hunting down a kid and dealing with some jerkwad in a house in the woods. But we're high-speed professionals. We'll handle it, and we'll look sharp while doing it.*

The leader's mouth moved. Roman read his lips: "Cute."

Aw, sweetness, if you think that's cute, you'll love what happens next.

The leader flicked his fingers. The SEAL-wannabe on his right with a full-on beard pulled a machete from a sheath on his waist and banged on the stop sign with it.

Knock, knock, knock.

"We have guests," Roman said.

Kor smiled, baring needle fangs.

The mercenary knocked again.

"I guess we'll have to go out and say hello. They came out all this way, we might as well be neighborly."

Kor stretched and hopped down. Roman picked up his coffee mug, stood up, and went out onto the porch.

The leader took in his ensemble of sweatpants, sweatshirt, and Eeyore slippers and gave him a big grin. "Hey there!"

"Can I help you gentlemen with something?" Roman took a gulp of his coffee.

"We're here for the boy and his dog."

No pleasantries. Straight to the point. They were certain the kid was in the house, and they were sure they could take him out of it.

"Is that so?" Roman asked.

"This doesn't have to be complicated," the leader said. "We're not going to hurt him. We're just going to take him back to his family. It's not safe for him to be running around the woods with the magic up."

"So he's a runaway?"

"He's a kid. He overreacted. His family is worried and wants him back."

Heh. "Do they now? And they hired you to bring him back? You get a lot of jobs finding lost kids?"

The leader shrugged. "You got me. This isn't something we normally do, but who am I to tell rich people what to do with their money? A job is a job."

"And you needed Honeycombers for it?"

The shorter of the trackers grinned. Honeycombers lived in a former trailer park warped by magic. Everyone with a crumb of common sense had moved out when the trailers started splitting like dividing cells. It was a place where people took a wrong step, walked into a wall, and were never seen again. Those who stayed remained because the Honeycomb was lawless, and they liked it that way.

The Honeycombers weren't picky about who paid them. They would do almost anything if the price was right. If you had to hire them, you were up to no good.

The leader smiled. "Whatever gets the job done. Look, you seem like a man who values his privacy. You live all the way out here, miles from town. You don't like to be bothered."

Nice how he worked that threat in there. *You live all alone and nobody will hear you scream.* Roman smiled into his coffee mug.

"Oh, I'm not bothered."

"Let us take the kid off your hands, and you can keep being not bothered and continue with your holiday decorating." The leader nodded at the half-finished Christmas tree. "It will be like we were never here."

Now that part was true.

"Sounds good. But I just have a few questions."

"Shoot."

Oh, I will. "What's the dog's name?"

The leader didn't say anything.

"See, finding runaways is one of the things I do. When a family wants their child back, they trip all over themselves trying to tell you everything about them. Before I leave the parents' house, I know the kid's middle name. I know their pets' names, their best friends, their grandmother's name and address. I know what they were wearing the last time they were seen and their favorite food."

The smugness slid off the leader's face.

"Given that you were hired to bring this kid back, I'm sure you know all that."

"Well, I'll level with you. I don't know the dog's name. Like I said, this isn't the kind of job we normally take."

"But a job is a job. Tell you what, send one of your guys down to Atlanta and bring the parents here. If they want him back, they'll make the trip. He's safe with me. He's not going anywhere. Once the parents show up, we'll take it from there."

The leader sighed. It was a resigned kind of sigh. He was clearly put upon. It didn't have to be like this. But now his hands were tied.

"You seem like a reasonable man. Do the math."

"It's not about math. And yes, normally I'm reasonable enough. But this is what you might call an emotionally difficult time of the year for me. I'm irritable, out of eggnog, and one of my free-loading creatures ate my cookies. You should leave while you still can."

"None of that is my problem. Last chance." The leader crossed his arms. "Send the kid out."

"You're right. This is your last chance. Leave now and every-body walks away alive."

"Why does it always have to be the hard way?" The leader nodded at the Honeycomb trackers. "Bring me his arms."

The shorter of the trackers dropped the lead of his iron hound. "Go on, Trigger. Get 'im! Get 'im!"

Trigger snarled. Foot-long iron spikes snapped erect on his spine. His fur stood on end. The huge canine bit the air and bounded forward. Two feet from the boundary of wards, he changed his mind and slid to a halt. The second dog, only a step behind, smacked into him, bounced off, and whined.

"Trigger! King! Get 'im!"

The dogs paced back and forth, unsure. Trigger turned around and looked at his handler.

"That's a clue for you," Roman said.

The shorter Honeycomber frowned. He was clearly having second thoughts.

The leader glanced at the handlers. "I'm waiting to get my money's worth."

A moment passed.

The thinner handler swore and pulled a club off his back. "Fuck it, I'll do it myself."

"Roscoe," the shorter handler said.

"I said, I'll do it myself."

The Honeycomber started forward. His eyes were bright. Roman knew that look. He'd seen it plenty of times before. Roscoe had left the Honeycomb and come all this way through the snow two days before Christmas. This wasn't just about the money. He wanted to have some fun.

Roman raised his left hand, palm up, as if he were holding an invisible apple. Dark tendrils of power sank through his feet, seeking and finding knots of ancient magic buried below.

The skinny Honeycomber took another step.

Roman clasped his hand into a fist.

A huge bone hand with wicked curved talons burst from the ground under Roscoe and clamped him in its skeletal fingers, jerking him off the ground. His feet dangled. His mouth gaped in a terrified *O*.

Roman squeezed.

Bones crunched with a crack. Roscoe's eyes rolled up, his head lolled, and he went limp.

Roman made a tossing motion.

The hand hurled the broken man off the property and toward the men on the road. They scattered, and he landed in the snow. The hand sank back into the ground.

The shorter Honeycomber dropped to his knees next to Roscoe and put his ear on the man's chest.

"Not dead," Roman said. "Just broken."

The shorter Honeycomber whistled a shrill note. The two iron hounds charged back to him. He heaved Roscoe onto King's back, reached into his shirt, pulled a bag out and dropped it in the snow.

"We had a deal," the leader said.

"This weren't no part of that deal. You wanted to find the kid. We found him. We're going home, Wayne."

"Suit yourself."

The Honeycomber turned.

"He's going to kill you," Roman said.

The Honeycomber whipped around.

Wayne nodded.

Six crossbows twanged in unison. One bolt took the Honeycomber in the throat, three more sprouted from Roscoe and King. The iron hound went down with a metallic clang like someone had dropped a bag of nickels. Two more bolts sank into Trigger, one into his back and another into his side. The big dog spun, looking for an exit, pinned between the fire team and the house.

The crossbowmen reloaded with ridiculous speed.

Trigger turned his head, his eyes desperate, looking at Roman. Their stares met.

Fine, what's one more? Roman nodded.

Trigger charged toward the house.

The two crossbowmen hiding on the flanks fired.

Two skeletal hands burst from the ground, lacing their fingers together in a protective cage around the porch. The bolts bounced off and fell to the snow. Trigger climbed the porch steps. Blood drenched his iron hide. Roman held the door open, and the dog sprinted into the house.

"It's like that then?" Wayne asked.

"It always was." Roman finished the last of his coffee. "You had your chance. Now none of you will leave here alive."

Wayne grinned. "And here I thought this would be a boring job. Sit tight. Don't go anywhere."

The team backed away from the property line and fanned out, melting into the woods.

THE DOG HAD COLLAPSED IN THE LIVING ROOM, RIGHT ON THE EDGE of the rug. The nechist pondered him, unsure. As Roman strode into the room, the melalo waddled over to the iron hound and slapped Trigger's nose with his wings.

"No hazing!" Roman snapped.

The melalo darted behind the couch.

"If he does that again, bite him."

The dog whined softly. Blood dripped from the two bolts embedded in his hide.

Roman knelt by him.

On the blankets, the kid lay unmoving. The German Shepherd had woken up and was watching Trigger. Didn't get up to get a sniff though. Interesting.

"We're going to do this quick."

Roman grasped the shaft of the bolt sticking out of the dog's back and jerked it free. The dog snarled.

"Hey, you came to me, remember? You ran into the house. Just one more."

Roman grabbed the other bolt and yanked it out. The dog jerked and whined but didn't snap.

Outside, twilight had fallen, and the fireplace didn't illuminate much, but he served the god of darkness. His night vision was better than a cat's. Darkness was home, shelter, and friend, and if he needed light, he could always make his own.

Roman turned the bolt over in his hand, examining the arrowhead. A black Annihilator broadhead, steel, shaped like a triangle cut out of a circle with convex curves. Reusable, durable, could be resharpened in the field. Most bolt heads cut slits into the target. This one punched holes.

He turned the shaft. A spidery script wrapped around the bolt, written in silver permanent marker. This was a military incantation, designed to activate once the bolt launched from the crossbow. He'd wondered why it cut through the dog's iron fur like it was butter.

None of the jokers that had come up to the house looked like active Military Supernatural Defense Unit personnel, and even if they had been at one time, using military incantations on civilian bolts was against the law. Most likely one of the local MSDU mages was moonlighting, selling enchanted bolts to the highest bidder. Or maybe they had a veteran who'd retired.

Roman clicked his tongue. This was a good deed that begged to be punished.

But the dog required attention first.

"Let's see if you qualify for the Black Volhv special." Roman set the bolt aside, rubbed his hands together, and cracked his fingers.

Magic swirled around his fingers, clinging to them like dense smoke. His mouth shaped the Russian words, suffusing them with power.

"Oh, Chernobog, God of Bone,
In the name of Darkness, in the name of the Final End,
Grant your creature your strength,
Heal the wounds and make it whole."

The darkness slipped from his fingers, clutched the dog, and seeped into the open wounds. The flesh knitted itself closed.

Roman petted the dog's head. "Congratulations. You're evil enough."

The dog stared at him, puzzled.

Evil in the pagan world was a relative term. Evil in the human world was not.

The window in the kitchen creaked, and a tiny bird flew into the room and perched on the table. Kor flicked his ears. Roman looked at him. The korgorusha closed his eyes into mere slits.

The bird shifted from foot to foot. It was barely five inches long, with gray on its back, a white throat and belly, and a cap of light, reddish brown.

"Dobry wieczór," Roman said.

The brown-headed nuthatch opened his beak and Dabrowski's voice came out. "Good evening to you, too. Look at you, a full menagerie."

Yeah, he was one to talk. "Is that a new bird?"

"He's Popper's son, from last year's clutch." The druid's voice vibrated with pride.

"Very handsome."

"He is. And such a good boy."

"What brings you to my neck of the woods?"

"Some heavily-armed dickheads showed up at my place asking about you."

Well, at least someone on that crew had some brains. A smart soldier did his recon. "What did you tell them?"

"I mostly talked about how I love my trees while braiding my vines into fancy shapes around them. Trees need good fertilizer, you see. And human bodies make really good fertilizer. Very nutritious when properly processed. I also mentioned that I personally don't bother you unless it's absolutely necessary."

"Thanks," Roman said.

"Do you need help?"

"Nah. I've got this."

The kid's eyelashes trembled slightly.

"Let me know if you change your mind. Last I saw, they were going up the road to see Schatten next."

"Really? Why would they do that?"

The little bird laughed. "I may have sent them that way."

Yes, and Ludwig would love that. "You know how he enjoys visitors."

"Oh yes, he's a regular Martha Stewart, that one. The soul of hospitality."

A distant blast thundered.

"They found Schatten!" The druid cackled.

"Damn it." Roman frowned.

"What?"

"I owe him twenty bucks. I told him that magically rigging those IEDs would never work."

"That was a sucker's bet. Well, I'm off. Whistle if you need something."

The bird hopped up and flew back to the kitchen and out the window.

"It's hard to lie there without moving," Roman said. "I know you're awake. You might as well throw in the towel."

The boy sat up. The shepherd sat in front of him, putting herself between the boy and Roman.

Trigger turned to look at the kid, his iron fur ringing with a metallic jangle, and the little puppy bared her teeth.

"Let's start with who you are and why people are chasing you?"

The boy didn't answer. His mouth was a hard, flat line across his face.

"Don't feel like talking?"

No answer.

Roman sighed. Story of his life. "Well, it is what it is. The die is cast. For whatever reason, I decided not to let them have you, so you are stuck here with me. Unless you want to make my life easier and walk out to the welcoming committee outside?"

The boy shook his head.

"Do you have a name, or is that a secret?"

"Finn."

"And lo, he opens his mouth and sounds come forth." Roman shook his head. "Do I need to let someone know where you are? Is anybody worried about you? Did you run away from home?"

"No."

"Is that no to a particular question or to all three?"

"No to all three. My sister will find me. She will come for me."

"Oh, good. Then we'll just have to wait for your sister. But you must understand one thing. Some of the people tracking you can't track anyone anymore. That's a heavy burden. If I have to start taking lives, we'll revisit this conversation. Killing cannot be done lightly, and I'll need to know why I'm doing it."

No response.

"Are you hungry?" Roman asked.

Finn nodded.

"Well, let's get you and your hound fed."

[3]

Roman pulled the smaller pot off the stove and set it on a trivet. "Hand me that stack of bowls over there, will you?"

Finn brought the bowls over. Roman lifted the lid and scooped the rice, cubed venison, and soft veggie mess into the top bowl and handed it to Finn. The boy looked at the food, clearly torn between hunger and being grossed out.

"It's not for you. This is for Trigger. And this smaller one is for your puppy."

Finn blinked. "Can dogs have carrots?"

"Dogs are omnivores. Carrots are good for them, and these two need a quick punch of energy to recover, so some brown rice will do them good, too. Now cats are a different story."

Smoke swirled, and Kor popped into existence on the table, his long, fluffy tail curling around the bowls.

Roman waved at him. "Off the table."

Kor purred.

"What kind of cat is he?" Finn asked.

"Kor isn't a cat. He's a korgorusha. They have a mind of their own, like cats. When they love you, they protect your house and property and bring you presents they steal from the neighbors.

When they're mad at you, they'll claw your pillows and break your dishes."

Roman ran his hand along Kor's soft back, sending a bit of smoke curling up from his black fur, worked his fingers under the front left paw, and raised it. Wicked claws shot out of the fur and curled around his finger. "Iron claws."

The kid opened his eyes wide. "Really?"

"No. But they might as well be. They're magic. There is no cutting these. You'd need a hoof trimmer. Trust me, when he claws someone, they know it."

Kor purred louder, his eyes small glowing slits.

Roman gave him another pet.

"Are you going to feed him?"

"He takes care of his own food. But I'm going to treat him."

Roman pulled a bottle of milk out of the refrigerator, poured a bit into a bowl, and set it in front of the korgorusha. "Feed the dogs, Finn. We feed the animals first, then we feed ourselves."

The boy took the two bowls into the living room.

Kor lapped the milk.

Roman brought a sack of chicken feed out, poured it into the long trough he used for the kolovershi, spooned some rice and meat into it, stirred it, set it on the floor, and knocked on the table. The kolovershi flew from the living room, gliding from their hidden perches, past Finn as he was returning to the kitchen, and for a moment he was caught inside the flock. Finn froze. The kolovershi landed in the kitchen and scurried over to their dinner.

"What are they?"

"Kolovershi and kolovertishi. Witch helpers. When a witch or a koldun, a sorcerer, starts working their magic, they attract these guys. They just come out of the woodwork. They feed on magic, and they are what they eat, so each pack is a little different. Some look like rabbits, some look more like owls. These weirdoes are mine."

The melalo waddled over to the trough.

"What about the bird?" Finn asked.

"Him." Roman grimaced. "He's a melalo, a Romani disease demon. Unclean creatures don't have the best origin stories. Some are born from muck, some from corrupted witch spit, but he takes the cake. He's the product of the most vile, sick shit that will turn your stomach."

"That bad?"

"Mhm. Take it from me, kid. You don't need that story in your life. Now, he is supposed to be much more powerful than he is."

The melalo gulped the feed, choked, and kept eating.

"I don't know why the hell he is like this. Maybe because one of his heads died or maybe not enough people believe in him anymore."

"You don't like him." Finn tilted his head.

"I don't."

"Why do you have him if he's that bad then?"

"He showed up on my doorstep half-dead, crawled to my boot, and clung to it. What was I supposed to do, toss him into the garbage?"

Roman poured a little more milk into another bowl and set that on the floor. The cabinet door under the sink opened, and the anchutka crawled out and headed for it.

"And this one?"

"An anchutka. They get a bad rep, but they are just small magic critters. Similar to lesser fae. Don't like salt or iron. Mostly keep to themselves. They only get agitated when people encroach on their territory, and even then, all they do is try to scare you with eerie noises and stare at you from the darkness. They're cowards. After this one eats, she will crawl back into her cabinet and we won't see her until everything is over."

A low whine rolled through the house.

"And that?"

"That's Roro. Roro will get to come out after everyone eats. If I let her out now, she'll tear through here like a wrecking ball, and I don't have time to clean up that mess."

Roman took another pot off the stove and ladled out two bowls of stew. He'd made a big pot yesterday. With his mood getting worse and worse, he knew he wouldn't feel like cooking. Warming up the leftovers for the next three days would be about all he was capable of. Except now things had shifted.

"This is for us. Venison and wild mushrooms. Don't give any to your dog. Mushrooms aren't good for her."

They took their food into the living room. Finn sat on the couch, brought the first spoonful to his lips, tasted it, and began shoveling the stew into his mouth. He mustn't have eaten for a couple of days, but he'd fed the nechist first without complaining. Maybe there was something to this kid.

Roman walked over to the window. Night had fallen, the snow a ghostly blue blanket on the ground. He concentrated. The darkness parted before his eyes. The mercenary assholes had gone to ground just beyond the property line. They were checking their crossbows.

"Our friends are thinking of invading." He tasted the stew. Mmmm, good. His appetite was back. How about that?

Finn raised his head from his bowl.

"Let's see if we can't discourage them a bit."

Roman twisted his left hand in their air, reshaping the magic, and gave it a push. A ball of blue fire shot out from his chest through the window and unfurled about ten feet above the snow, flowing into a six-foot-tall skull made of magic glow. The skull's lower jaw swiveled as if laughing. The four sabertooth fangs on the top and bottom rows cracked against each other loudly.

The mercenaries hit the snow in unison.

The skull exploded into a dozen spheres of ball lightning. The shining clumps streaked in a semicircle and broke against skull torches that slid out of the ground. The carved skulls atop the eight-foot poles ignited, bathing the front yard in an eerie neon light. One of the balls perched atop the Christmas tree. Roman pulled a bit more magic from it and scattered small bits of glow throughout the branches.

Nice.

Finn's jaw hung open.

"Fancy, no?" Roman chuckled.

Finn remembered to close his mouth.

The mercenaries stayed down. Heh. *That's right, enjoy the snow.*

"Is that so you could see them?" Finn asked.

"It's so they can see each other. I don't need light. I know exactly where they are."

"I don't get it," Finn said.

"They thought they would be slick and sneak up on me in the dark. Now the yard is lit up, so they don't have cover anymore."

Roman dropped into a chair and started on his stew.

"But couldn't you just pick them off in the darkness?"

"I could," Roman agreed. "But I told you, taking a human life comes with a cost. You should only kill when you have no choice."

Finn had stopped eating. He was looking into the fire, lost in thought.

"What is it?" Roman asked.

"Your god is an evil god."

"Chernobog is a dark god, technically."

"When you healed the dog, you told him he was evil enough. You didn't heal me with that magic because I'm not evil enough."

"It's more complicated than that, but go on, make your point."

"Why take care of all these creatures? Why not sacrifice them? Why wouldn't you kill those people out there? Shouldn't that be something your god would like?"

Roman sighed. "You're confusing darkness and death with the profoundly immoral. The Slavic pagan world has three parts, the Tri-world, made up of Yav, Nav, and Prav. Yav is the realm of humans. Prav is where the light, good gods live; deities like Svarog the Smith, God of Fire, and Belobog, God of Light and Creation.

Then there is Nav, the death realm, where the dark, evil gods dwell. My god is Chernobog, Belobog's twin. God of Darkness and Death. Do you know what's beyond Nav?"

Finn shook his head.

"Chaos. The end of everything. Nav is the realm that protects us from that." Roman ate another spoonful. "The name of the game is balance. Crops are planted in the spring, they grow, they are harvested, and then winter comes. Their roots and stems decay and nourish the earth. Chernobog is the one who makes that decay happen. As the remnants of the crops die, the soil rests and rejuvenates. Without winter, without the Goddess Morena, Chernobog's wife and consort, there cannot be spring. One cannot just take and take. One must give back."

The logs crackled in the fire. The two dogs had finished their food and sprawled in front of the fireplace, satisfied. Three of the mercenaries had taken off down the road, back the way they'd come. Now where were they headed?

"People don't like death. It scares them, so they call Chernobog evil. Winter is hard, so they call Morena evil. Disease and sickness are cruel and unforgiving, so they call Troyan the Healer, a Nav god, evil because sometimes no matter how much you pray to him, he doesn't answer. But we are crops, Finn. We must grow, thrive, flourish, and die, to make room for other living creatures. Such is life. So no, I won't be going on a murder spree for the sake of killing. To Chernobog, every life out there has value. I will take if I must. But I won't be the one to upset the balance first."

The kid had forgotten about his food again. Something was bothering Finn. Roman could almost feel the wheels turning in his head.

All in good time. Patience was something he had in abundance.

A knot of magic ignited on the edge of the property, and it had a particular flavor. Not Abrahamic, not pagan... But something else. Definitely a divine derivative. And a light divine, too.

40

The mercenaries were back, and they had brought someone else with them.

The magic flared.

Couldn't even let him finish a bowl of stew in peace. Roman rose and took his staff from where it rested against the wall.

Klyuv opened its beak and shrieked.

"Brace yourself," Roman told Finn. "I think we're about to get attacked with some goodness and light."

THE KNOT OF MAGIC SPUN, CHURNING, JUST ON THE EDGE OF Roman's senses. The source of it was hidden behind the trees. The mercenaries were keeping it well outside of his reach. If he shut his eyes and let his mind take over, the knot of magic blazed, bright white, like an angry star.

Whoever that was, they were idling way too high. Whipping that much magic through one's body was bad for you. It cut down on your lifespan.

Roman tapped the floor with his staff. "Vasya. I need you."

Deep within the cold ground, a presence stirred, drowsy and unwilling.

"I know, I know."

He should've been asleep, digesting the rabid bear he'd eaten two days ago, but sometimes things couldn't be helped.

Vasya shuddered and started forward, toward the dirt plugging up the entrance to his lair's underground tunnel.

The leader of the mercenaries walked into the open. Behind him, a pair of armed men walked a blindfolded man between them. He was of average height, with a mane of long, wavy dark hair pulled back from his face into a half ponytail.

"Who is that?" Finn asked.

"A priest of some sort."

"Why is he blindfolded?"

"That's a good question."

The small group halted just outside the property line.

"So whose priest is he?" Finn asked.

"We won't know until he invokes."

"What's that?"

"Invoking is when you beg your god to cover that really big check your fool mouth just wrote."

"Can you invoke?"

"My god is having family issues right now. Not a good time."

Finn squinted at the priest. "What happens if the god doesn't answer?"

"You're fucked."

"Mr. Roman!" The mercenary leader called out.

And they had learned his name. Dabrowski must've let it slip. If they had done a background check, they would've called him by his last name, Tihomirov.

Roman looked at Finn. "Stay here. Don't come out."

The kid nodded.

Roman walked out onto the porch.

"I think we've gotten off on the wrong foot," the merc said. "My name is Wayne Greene. I own Shadow Strike Solutions."

So awesome. So impressive. *I've got some shadows for you, buddy. Don't you worry.*

"These are my people. They are all good, solid guys. I run a clean operation. I like to do things above board."

You don't say.

"It wouldn't sit right with me if I didn't give you this last chance to avoid bloodshed. The optics of this are bothering me. My team is about to take down a lone man and his pets in a single house in the middle of the woods. There is no glory here. They won't sing songs about this one in Valhalla."

Ah. A neo-Viking. A lot of mercenaries skewed Norse. The idea of being rewarded and celebrated for their lives of violence appealed to them. Instead of seeing themselves as paid muscle-

42

for-hire, they preferred to envision themselves as wolves and reavers in human skin, seeking glory in the name of a higher calling. When one of them died in battle, instead of dealing with the grim reality of replacing him with the next warm body and sending his family his last check, they would make speeches, drink, and growl about seeing their brother in the mead halls of Valhalla.

"So, what are you going to do about it?" Roman asked.

"A man's home is his castle. You want to protect it. I understand that. In your place, I'd do the same. Nobody likes a pack of random strangers showing up on their doorstep and making demands. That's why I'm going to make you an offer instead. Before I unleash hell, I must at least try."

Ah. Personnel management. This wasn't about him. This was about Wayne looking good in front of his crew. They saw themselves as elite. Attacking a peaceful man in his house and child trafficking didn't exactly go with the whole glorious warrior shtick. But Wayne had taken the money, and now he was giving himself an out in case any of them grumbled about this incident later.

Oh, it's such a shame we had to kill that deranged hermit in the woods. Poor guy. I gave him a chance to save himself, I tried to be reasonable, I warned him. If only he had listened to me.

"Let me level with you," Wayne said.

"Oh, please do."

"I'm willing to compensate you for the inconvenience. How much will it take to resolve this matter peacefully today?"

"Finn?" Roman called out.

"Yes?" Finn asked from inside the house.

"Are you here of your own free will?"

"Yes."

"Do you want to go with these men?"

"No. I don't."

Roman stared at Wayne. Seconds ticked by.

"What's your answer?" Wayne finally said.

"I'm waiting for you to say it out loud. Say 'how much money will it take for us to buy a child and drag him out of your house?' Listen to the words as you say them and then explain to me again how you are the good guys here."

The faces of the two mercenaries behind Wayne told Roman that one had landed.

"It's not like that," Wayne said.

"I know your gods. I've met Odin." And what a memorable, super fun meeting that had been. If he never saw another Norse god in his lifetime, it would be too soon. "They do not celebrate slavers in neo-Valhalla."

That one also landed.

"What you're really asking," Roman said, "is the price of my soul. But I can't sell it to you. It's already claimed. All the money in the world would not make me give you this kid."

Wayne heaved a sigh. "I fucking tried."

"Yes, yes. Do what we both know you were going to do anyway."

The mercenary leader spun around and jerked the blindfold off the priest's face. The man stared at Roman with dark eyes. That was a hell of a thousand-yard stare. He didn't seem to know where he was. The magic inside him had swelled like a raging river straining against a dam.

Wayne leaned to the priest and pointed at Roman. "Look, Farhang. Evil!"

Awareness sparked in Farhang's eyes. A sluice gate had opened, and the chaotic maelstrom of his power had found a target.

Shit.

Roman planted his staff onto the porch.

Light exploded from Farhang, rolling like a blast wave, shaking the snow off the trees. It smashed into the staff and broke on its shaft, rattling Klyuv in Roman's fingers. The house shook behind him. Inside Roro howled with an unearthly voice.

Farhang turned his hands downward and spun them.

What are you?

A loud, triumphant chant spilled from the priest's lips. Unfamiliar words, a foreign language, channeling power. The snow swirled around him, mixing with golden light.

Finn stepped outside.

"Get back," Roman told him.

"No."

The light coalesced into rings that slid up and down around Farhang with an electric strumming sound. *Whoosh. Whoosh. Whoosh.* He was like a volcano about to blow.

The kid raised his head and took a deliberate step closer to Roman.

"What are you doing?" Roman growled.

"Being a human shield."

"Do what now?"

"They won't hit you if I stand close." Finn edged a little closer.

Farhang clapped his hands. "...*Ahura...*!"

Oh, fuck it all.

Roman grabbed Finn and yanked him to the floor of the porch.

Missiles of golden fire erupted out of Farhang and streaked toward the house.

The bone hands burst from the ground, clamping together into a shield. The golden fireballs hammered into them. The skeletal shield shook under the barrage, sizzling from the impact.

Inside the house Roro yowled like a demon.

Of all the denominations, it had to be *that* one. What did those svolochi do to him? Had to be something really potent. A restricting amulet would've emitted its own magic, but Farhang was putting out so much power it was hard to sense anything in that blinding light.

"What the hell is he?" Finn squeezed out.

"Get into the house!"

"I will shield you! They want me alive!"

"He didn't get that memo, kid. Inside. Now!"

Slivers of bone peppered the floorboards as the light struck chunks from the bone fingers. Finn scrambled into the house on all fours, landed just inside the doorway, and stayed there.

The mercenaries advanced in a ragged line. He could see them through the gaps in the damaged fingers, eight figures carefully moving in, Wayne in the middle, in the second line. The two shooters remained in their spots on the flanks, waiting for the right moment to put a bolt in his chest.

Beneath the ground Vasya waited, wrapped in dark magic and feeling put out.

Not yet.

The barrage finally died.

Roman peered at the battlefield. Farhang was back in his powering-up pose. The golden rings coalesced and began their up-and-down dance.

Whoosh. Whoosh. Whoosh.

He was going to do it again. If this kept going, the man's heart might give out.

Farhang's eyes were still blank. Focused but blank. He was on autopilot, like an automated Gatling gun. Which meant he would alternate between the two main weapons in his arsenal that were consistent with his faith. He'd done the purifying fire. That left the other option. Now to nudge him toward it…

Okay, so yes, let's do that.

Roman pushed the bone hands apart with his magic, pivoting them open, thrust his staff at the advancing line, and snarled a command suffused with magic. *"Imenem Chernoboga!"*

Not a true invocation but impressive enough.

Klyuv opened its beak. A swarm of black flies the size of grapes shot out from the staff's mouth like a black cloud, spiraled, and fell onto the mercenaries. The Shadow Strikers cursed, waving their arms. The flies wouldn't kill, but they stung like hell.

Farhang stared at the flailing mercs.

Cleanse them.

Cleanse them.

Farhang rotated his hands. The light rings broke into a glowing wide spiral, picking up snow from the ground. The light-infused snow tornado spun and melted in an instant, turning into a waterspout. The water funnel burst. Glowing water drenched the mercenaries and the flies. Tiny black bodies rained on the ground.

Perfect.

Roman smashed the staff into the porch, driving a spike of pure power into Klyuv, through the shaft, and into the ground below. A phantom cold sprang from him like a magic river and sped through the ground, branching as it flowed. Black ice stabbed through the soil and snow, mirroring the river's course, and clamped the mercenaries into its bear trap, locking them in place. Even holy cleansing water was still water. It froze, especially when fed with Chernobog's ice on his consecrated ground.

He had to give it to Wayne's crew. They didn't scream.

Wayne jerked a machete from its sheath and hacked at the ice that shackled his shins. "I need fire, Farhang!"

Roman sent an icy mote down below. *Now.*

A crossbow bolt tore out of the tree line and sliced across his left thigh in a hot burn. The snipers. Damn it.

Roman clenched his fist. The lights went out. Darkness drowned the front yard. Farhang stood alone, illuminated by his golden light.

A deep human howl tore through the night.

Another.

Fire erupted from Farhang's fingertips, pummeling the darkness at random.

Roman stepped back, whipping the gloom around himself,

47

clothing his body in it like a shroud. It whetted his eyes and the night opened before him, clear as day. Three mercs and Wayne had broken free and hightailed it back to the woods at top speed. Four others remained anchored. Of those, the one on the right was missing a head, his body still locked upright by the ice, and a second one sprawled on the ground. The last two mercs twisted, one frantically hacking at the ice and the other swinging his short sword at the darkness.

Behind Roman, the door swung open. Finn stepped onto the porch, holding a crossbow, raised it, and leveled it at Farhang, who was bathed in his purifying fire like a torch.

"No!" Roman slapped the crossbow down.

"He's trying to kill us!"

"He isn't in his right mind."

A big, chitin-sheathed body burst from the ground. Huge pincers cut like chitin shears and sliced the merc on the left in half.

"Farhang!" Wayne snarled from midway down the driveway. "Do something!"

Farhang clenched his fists. The magic swelled inside him and tore out like a geyser, sending a ball of searing fire ten feet into the air. The tiny sun flooded the front yard, incinerating the darkness in an instant.

Pain lashed Roman with a burning whip, setting fire to his bone marrow, cooking his eyes in his head, steaming his brain. His insides clenched, and he vomited onto the porch.

Magic backlash was a bitch.

The midnight dawn blazed, furious and vivid, making every snowflake stand out.

The last merc looked around, realizing he was the only one left standing. The ground in front of him exploded outward, and a cow-sized black scorpion lunged out, huge, segmented tail striking. The merc shuddered, impaled by the spike. His eyes rolled back in his head, and he went limp.

The remaining Shadow Strikers stared, shocked.

Vasya locked two of the bodies with his pinchers and dove back underground, taking his dinner with him.

"Fucking kill that bastard!" Wayne howled.

Farhang shoved the ball of light at Roman. He saw it coming, and the familiar rage that always fed him when he'd been beaten down reared its ugly head.

Not today. Not fucking ever. Not in my own house.

Roman planted his feet and thrust the staff in front of him. His body opened, like a door, no longer just a physical form, but a conduit to elsewhere, a place without light, a realm of cold, where power lay waiting. He welcomed it. It filled him, packed itself into a huge, clawed fist, and smashed into the ball of light.

Magic clashed in a burst of purple lightning. The world shook.

The clawed hand squeezed the searing flame ball. It popped and went out.

Blood poured from Farhang's nose and mouth. His eyes rolled back in his head, and he went down like a sack of potatoes.

The torches bordering the yard flared with blue fire.

With a blood-curdling howl, Roro tore out of the front door, bounded across the yard, locked her jaws on Farhang's side, heaved him like he weighed nothing, galloped back to the porch, and dragged him into the house.

Roman swung his cloak of darkness around him, pushed Finn through the door, and went in after him. The last thing he saw was the stunned look on Wayne's face.

[4]

The problem with dramatic exits was that they cost a couple of seconds, so by the time he got back into the house, the nechist had managed to drag the unconscious priest down the hallway and toward her room.

Roman thrust Klyuv against the wall and stomped down the main hallway.

"Drop him!"

Roro shook her head, flinging a limp Farhang back and forth. The priest's head smacked into the wall. Great, now he'd be concussed on top of befuddled.

Roman charged into the kitchen, flung the fridge open, grabbed the beef shank bone he'd saved for soup, and ran back to the main hallway. Roro was trying to drag Farhang through the utility room doorway, toward her lair.

"Trade!"

Roro sighted the shank bone. Her jaws fell open, and Farhang crashed to the floor.

"*Roro?*"

Roman tossed the bone at Roro. She leapt three feet up, snatching it from the air, and took off toward the utility room.

The door swung closed behind her, moved by the draft. A massive hole gaped in the bottom. She'd chewed her way out.

Great. Now there would be no stopping her, and he'd have to replace the door.

Roman nodded at Finn. "Grab his legs."

Together they picked up Farhang and carried him into the living room, in front of the fire.

"Kor!" Roman called.

The korgorusha materialized on Farhang's chest, purring.

"Keep him napping," Roman ordered.

Smoke curled from Kor's black fur, swirling around Farhang. Korgorushas couldn't knock you out, but if you were drowsy and fell asleep, they could keep you sleeping for a while.

Finn stared at Farhang. "Why did you save him?"

"He's a Zoroastrian. Remember all that stuff I said about balance? Zoroastrians are the opposite of that. There is *asha*, the force of good and truth that comes from Ahura Mazda, and *druj*, the force of evil and falsehood that originates from Angra Mainyu, better known as Ahriman. The two are in constant battle, and every Zoroastrian is a soldier in that war. It is the sacred duty of the mobeds, the Zoroastrian priests, to eradicate evil in all its forms."

Finn squinted at Farhang. "So he is a mobed?"

"No. That is a real live magav. Very rare. The Greeks call them the magi."

"Like in the Bible?"

"Like in the Bible. He is a Magus. That's where the word *magic* comes from."

A weird cold was spreading through his thigh.

"Farhang isn't just a priest, he is a warrior-mage, a holy knight devoted to the protection of good. No force in this world would ever make him attack a child. If he were in his right mind, he would've asked a lot of questions before starting any fireworks, and he sure as hell wouldn't have let those assholes drag him around blindfolded. Something was done to him to make him like this…"

A spike of pain hammered through Roman's thigh, biting into the bone.

Roman yanked at the leg of his sweatpants, exposing the ragged cut where the bolt had grazed him. The wound had turned a weird olive-brown.

"Fucking assholes,"

He spun around and marched to the utility room. Finn chased him.

"What's wrong?"

"Poison." He stabbed his finger at the flock of kolovershi trailing him. "Bring me that bolt."

The kolovershi took off.

Roman tore into the room, flung a second fridge open, and rummaged through the gathering of glass vials on the shelves. *No, no, yes, no…*

He thrust a baggie with powdered herbs at Finn. "Hold this."

The boy took it. Panic shivered in his eyes.

Roman pulled a jar of Remedy out, scooped out some, and smeared it on the cut.

One, two, three… Still cold and hurting. And now it was climbing up, toward his kidneys. For Nav's sake…

He pushed vials aside, grabbed a green one, a blue one, and one with thick black goo, and shoved them all at Finn. The kid took them all with trembling fingers.

Roman slapped the fridge door shut and marched into the living room. The kolovershi pack swept into the room, and a bolt landed in his hand, still wet with his blood.

"Give me that bag." His voice was ragged. Pain bit into his gut.

Finn held out the baggie. Roman took it, pulled it open, and shook a handful of herbs into his palm. His fingers cramped. He forced his hand to close and clamped the bolt in his hand, plastering the herbs onto the bloody metal.

A small, fluffy-looking koloversh shivered, flinging snow off his feathery fur, and opened his mouth.

"*Call the client,*" the little koloversh snarled in Wayne's voice.

"*Wayne, we just lost half our team. You're not thinking of giving back the money, because we've got to pay out the death benefits...*"

Roman muttered an incantation under his breath.

"*Fuck no, we're not giving back the money. Call the fucking client. This wasn't how the job was sold to us, so if he wants it done, he's gonna have to pay us a hell of a lot more. Tell him he gives us more money, or we walk. If he has a problem with it, he can get on site and see what we're dealing with. And after that, call Fulton and tell him to get his ass and our antimage squad down here. This whole fucking job has been a shit show and that ends now.*"

The pain had climbed into his chest.

"*It's going to take all night for them to get here from Columbus.*"

"*Then they better get a fucking move on.*"

"*We should've done that when the skulls came on,*" a third voice growled. "*But no, you went all gung-ho because a pagan priest didn't roll over for you.*"

"*Not right now, Pike. Don't fucking test me.*"

The koloversh shut his mouth.

The last words of the incantation fell from Roman's lips. Magic sank into the bolt head like the fangs of a striking snake.

"Poison me, you zaraza." He hurled the bolt into the fire.

A howl of pain ripped through the night. One sniper down.

Roman pointed at the little koloversh. "Fedya, good boy. Finn, no matter what happens, stay inside the house. The rest of you, protect the kid."

He plucked the blue vial from Finn's fingers and gulped the liquid antidote. It burned through him like fire and crashed against the cold stabbing into his heart. He grabbed the green vial, drank it in one swallow, and twisted the cap off the black goo.

"Nobody panic. I'll be back."

He turned the vial upside down. The congealed drop of Chernobog's tear fell onto his tongue.

Darkness rose and swallowed him whole.

THE SNOW CRUNCHED UNDER HIS FEET, PRISTINE AND WHITE, LIKE the sugar glaze on a paska. The Milky Way glinted across the dark sky, clothed in magic, a brilliant backdrop to the full moon, unnaturally bright. Its gauzy light played over the woods, and the snowdrifts glittered as if dusted with crushed diamonds.

Around him pines towered, their fluffy needles perfectly still. Their scent floated in the air, a crisp, tangy fragrance, at once nostalgic and fleeting.

It smelled like Koliada.

His hands were free this time, but the pull across his chest assured him that the weight was still there, attached to him.

Of course. He hadn't finished dragging the damn tree yet. The moment he'd passed out, Chernobog had put him right where he'd left off, and he must've gone right back to pulling, unaware he was doing it.

When he chose to enter Nav on his own, he was instantly conscious. When Chernobog summoned him from a dream, however, awareness became a divine privilege. Sometimes he was aware, and sometimes he came to and found he'd been sitting by Chernobog's throne for hours in a catatonic state, his physical body in the human world, his metaphysical presence in Nav, while his mind was blissfully dreaming.

You single-minded bastard.

Roman felt the dark cloud of irritation rising inside him. Chernobog's tear suffused him with divine power, purging all poisons and ailments. A last resort, it packed a wallop that always knocked him out for about an hour. An hour Finn had to spend defending the house on his own, but only an hour. He should've woken up long ago.

Roman glanced over his shoulder. The massive tree lay on the snow behind him. Past it, through a gap in the pines, he could see a vast field rolling out to the horizon, where the jagged wall of another forest rose. He had dragged the tree past the firs of the Twilight Forest, past the Grueling Field, and was now in the Evening Woods. He had been in here for hours.

"Seriously? Did you not see I had my hands full? It's your marriage. Your wife is mad at *you*, not me. Why the hell am I involved in it?"

The woods didn't answer him.

Roman swore and checked himself. A harness woven out of a strange dark leather crossed his chest, looping over his shoulders. He was bound to the tree like a burlak, a barge puller from Russia's old past, a human beast of burden dragging the trade ships up the river. This forest was his personal towpath.

"So now I am an ox? Is that where we are? I am to drag the tree like a mindless animal?"

The night remained silent.

"You know what, fuck right off. I'm your beck-and-call boy for 362 days out of the year. I don't complain. I do whatever the fuck you want, no matter what is happening in my life. I'm with a nice girl, I think it's going well. I wake up in my kitchen standing in my own piss. The girl is gone. Never see her again. That's okay. I read the fine print before I signed. I knew what I was in for. I just do it. I always do it. I always do whatever you want even if it's stupid. I am supposed to get Koliada off. Three fucking days out of the year when you don't fucking bother me. I am off."

The trees remained silent.

"You know what, I'm going to drag this tree to you, and then I am done. I quit. Kill me, I don't give a fuck."

He started forward, stomping through the snow. The tree slid behind him like his personal ball and chain.

"Excuse me," a soft male voice said from his left, his tone tentative and cautious. "Can you see me?"

Roman glanced to the side. Farhang floated next to him, levitating about four feet off the ground in a classic cross-legged pose. He wore a white layered robe, pinned to his waist by a golden sash. White cloth wrapped around the top of his head, leaving his long dark hair to fall loose on his shoulders. He was clean-shaven, free of dirt, and his body glowed weakly with a pale golden light.

"This is your answer?" Roman demanded.

Silence.

"I suppose not," Farhang murmured. If there ever was a need for a visual example of being crestfallen, he was it.

Roman sighed. "Hello, Farhang."

Farhang's eyes lit up. "You *can* see me, and you know me?"

"In a manner of speaking. I've met your body."

"Oh. Um, if it's not too forward... Do you happen to know where my body is right now?"

"In my house, in front of a fireplace. I have a magic beast sitting on you to keep you asleep."

"May I ask how I got into your house?"

He seemed a little fragile. Hitting him with *you showed up at my house to forcefully remove a child from my care* might have been too much. "You came with some mercenaries."

Farhang's face fell. "I did?"

"Mhm."

"And it wasn't a friendly visit?"

"No."

Farhang hesitated. "Did I hurt someone?"

"You gave it a very good try."

Farhang winced.

"It's all good. Nobody that mattered was injured." Roman kept moving forward. "I figured out something was wrong pretty much from the get-go, so your body is unharmed."

Mostly. Mostly unharmed. Roro had really sharp teeth.

"I'm very sorry. My deepest apologies."

"Apology accepted."

Roman marched forward. Farhang hung next to him, keeping pace.

"The woods are a nice change," Farhang said after a while. "There is something about the scent of fir trees and pines that touches the soul."

"It's primeval," Roman said.

"Yes. That's what it feels like."

"Pines are ancient. They evolved before flowers did, almost 200 million years ago. Flower aromas are layered and complex, while the scent of pine is a simple fragrance. Yet every human responds to it. We know it by some forgotten instinct."

Scents and memories were intertwined. It wasn't the pines' fault that the memories they conjured set his teeth on edge. He couldn't sink into that dark hole right now. He had company.

"Where do you usually float?" Roman asked.

"Over a grassy plain with distant snowcapped peaks in the background. I believe it's the landscape of Northern Iran. Somewhere near Sareyn, perhaps."

"Sounds picturesque."

"Oh, it is," Farhang nodded. "A grand landscape, very vast. Feels almost infinite. And very lonely."

"How long has it been since you spoke to another human?"

Farhang pondered it. "Three years? I think."

All gods were assholes.

"What happened?"

Farhang sighed. "I swore a holy oath to defeat someone in the name of my god. I was warned against swearing it, but things got dramatic, and I swore it anyway. There was a woman involved."

"Happens to the best of us," Roman said. A woman was the reason he was dragging this cursed tree. Morena and Chernobog rarely fought, but they must have clashed over something this time, because the tree was clearly an apology gift.

Farhang smiled. "I failed to keep my pledge. The oath splintered me in two. My body, with a sliver of my consciousness, is in the physical world. The rest of me is here, locked out."

Three years floating in solitude, without any idea what was happening to his body. *Yes, I get it, Dark One, point made. It could always be worse. I don't care. I'm still quitting.*

"Have you attempted to appeal?" Roman asked. "Three years is a long time."

"Unfortunately, the Triad is of the opinion that since I ignored the explicit warning and got myself into this predicament, it is up to me to pull myself out of it. So far, I haven't been successful."

Many years had passed since his divinity classes. Roman raked his brain, trying to remember the particulars of the Ahuric Triad. There was Ahura Mazda and two others... He was pretty sure one of them was the god of covenants. An oath was a covenant, a contract. As a magav, Farhang would be held to the strictest of standards.

"I couldn't help but overhear that you are angry with your patron deity," Farhang said.

"That's one way to put it."

"In my experience, gods are selfish. They don't always explain things, but they do love us, for we are their chosen."

"Love is too strong a word," Roman said. "They use us. We are the instruments of their will. They have a vested interest in keeping us alive, but should we perish, they will simply find another."

"True. Such is the nature of the job. My teacher told me once that for a person to become what we are, they must have the Servant's Heart. We are similar to physicians and soldiers. We seek to serve a greater good and to belong to something meaningful and grand, and we dedicate our lives to putting ourselves between others and danger."

"That is a noble way to look at it. The reality is dirtier and grimmer." Roman jabbed his thumb over his shoulder, pointing at the tree.

Farhang looked mournful. "Indeed." He opened his mouth to say something else but closed it instead.

"What?"

"How I wish I had a tree to pull. At least, there would be an end. A destination."

They fell silent. Roman crunched through the snow. In the distance an eerie wail soared to the sky and lingered, squeezing his throat.

"Don't you start!" Roman snapped. "I'll pull your feathers out!"

The wail cut off mid-note. The woods were once again quiet.

"I realize that we might not have started on the right foot," Farhang said. "But may I keep you company for a while?"

He hadn't quite managed to keep the desperate note from his tone.

"Company would be most welcome."

Tension eased from Farhang's shoulders.

"I have to warn you, you might not like what is waiting for us up ahead," Roman said. "We are in Nav, inside the Slavic pagan world of the darker gods. This is the Winter Cathedral, where the Earth sleeps, not dead but suspended in a restorative rest. It is an ancient place, born from fears as old as life itself. This path is a trial. Look behind us."

Farhang glanced over his shoulder.

"Those trees in the distance are the Twilight Forest, where the Wolves of Doubt and Uncertainty prowl. The open ground you see is the Grueling Field, where spirits of the punished plant and plow, but never reap or harvest. It is a place of thankless work, nourished by worries that have plagued humankind since farming began. A place where seedlings die from crippling frost and plants are felled by cruel winds. The pines around us are the Evening Forest, where the Birds of Regret and Missed Chances shriek and wail. Once we pass through it, we will enter the Glades of

Remembrance. They will make you relive your most painful memories."

It might have been the glow of the golden light, but the magav looked slightly paler.

"I will stay," he said.

"Suit yourself."

After a while the trees began to thin. Roman could almost glean the clearing ahead. Whether he liked it or not, he would see him. He had to brace himself.

"*Wake up!*"

The voice echoed through the woods. Finn's voice.

"*Wake up, wake up!*"

Something had gone pear-shaped again.

"Farhang, I'll be back. Wait for me here. Don't try to enter the Glades without me."

"I will stay right here by the tree," the magav promised. "You have my word."

[5]

Roman opened his eyes. Pale, early morning light filtered through the living room window and mixed with the glow from the fire. He'd been out all night.

Damn it all.

Roman sat up.

Farhang was still asleep, Kor lying on his chest. The korgorusha's eyes were fixed on the window. The iron hound, Roro, and the rest of the nechist had parked themselves by the glass, staring out with glowing eyes. Something bad was happening.

Even the kid's puppy sat with her nose glued to the window. Finn was nowhere to be found.

A male voice floated in from outside, too vague to distinguish the individual words, but he got the tone—condescending dickhead.

The shepherd puppy turned and looked at him over her shoulder. The dog's outline shimmered. For a blink, a different shape curled within the space, woven of darkness. He saw black feathers, a dusting of crystalline white, a flash of blood-red... Golden eyes stared at him, a glimpse of the Wild, ancient, cold, and forever untamable by humankind. It reached into his chest and squeezed his heart in its polar grip.

He spun within a snow whirlwind under the flames of green and purple godfire painted across the dark sky. Conifer needles brushed his skin, the heady scent of pine resin intoxicating and thick. The crack of glaciers snapping, the sound of ice growing, the whisper of snow falling, and the howl of winter wind drowned him, deafening, impossibly loud. He heard a wolf song, felt the heated sweat slick his body under furs as he chased survival across an icy plain, saw his own breath, and smelled blood as the hot arterial spray hit the snow. Life through death, a cycle never ending, a wheel ever turning... Godfire, ice, labored breath, blood, sacrifice, rebirth, spinning faster and faster...

It spat him back out into his living room.

His heart thawed. The taste of blood on his lips warmed him.

The little shepherd gazed at him with puppy eyes.

"Got it," he ground out. "I suspected. I don't care. I've already decided to help him. Not for you. For him."

He got up to his feet and went to the window.

Finn stood on the porch, rigid, his legs planted. He was holding Klyuv in his hand, and his fingers were bloody. The staff eyed him but let him hold it.

Across the front yard, at the other end of the property, a dark-haired asshole in combat fatigues and fingerless gloves held the melalo by his wing. The bird monster dangled from the man's fingers. Clean-shaven, trim, about the same height as Wayne standing next to him. Two peas in a pod.

The new guy wore an amulet around his neck. The number of soldiers-for-hire around his property had multiplied, too. The promised mage squad must've arrived during the night, and by the looks of it, they had been busy. Six ten-foot stakes rose just outside of the yard in a wide crescent, each carved with runes, and topped with a goat head staring at the house. They'd broken out the nithing poles.

Nithing poles were a curse conduit, but the entire property was consecrated as Chernobog's holy ground. A curse wouldn't affect it. The runes glowed with power, so they weren't complete amateurs. They had to have known that.

Roman pushed slightly. His power crept toward the poles and recoiled. Ah. Not a curse then. They had repurposed the nithing poles into a ward, shielding their position. Clever. Really clever.

Livestock was precious, and to curse something, you had to pay the price. The more valuable the animal, the more juice it gave the curse. Chickens were on the bottom rung of the ladder, goats and sheep were mid-range, and finally, horses and cows were top tier. They'd cheaped out a bit.

"Look kid," the mage dickhead said, "it's over. Your volhv friend has been shot by a viper bolt. Paralysis in forty-five minutes, coma in four hours, death in eight to twelve. I bet he's out cold, right? You tried to wake him up and you couldn't."

Finn's fingers gripped the staff so hard, the knuckles of his right hand were white.

"Here, hold this." The mage thrust the melalo at Wayne. Wayne grimaced but took the wing. The melalo was doing his best impression of roadkill, body limp, the one living head lulled to the side.

The mage reached into the pocket of his fatigues and pulled out a small vial filled with blue liquid.

"Antidote," the mage said slowly, pronouncing each syllable. "You can save him."

Finn clenched his teeth.

The mage shook his head. "You're not getting it. You have two choices here. Walk out, and we give the volhv the antidote and you leave with us. Or, we wait you out, he dies, we come in and slit the throat of everything that's still alive in that shack, burn the place, and you still leave with us. He lives, he dies. Doesn't matter to me."

That *shack*?

Wayne put his hand out in a restraining gesture. The mage gave him a look.

"He is a kid, Fulton," Wayne told him.

The mage rolled his eyes. "You wanted me here because you couldn't get the job done. I dragged my ass out here. But it's your show. Go ahead. Just a small suggestion, if I may?"

Wayne made a go-ahead gesture.

"We are due at the Lumber City job in twenty hours. That's not a lot of turnaround time, and none of my guys have had any sleep. It's one kid, a pack of magical vermin, and one dying pagan priest. What if we just wrap this up and maybe still catch a little downtime?"

Wayne might have outranked Fulton, but judging by the caliber of the wards, the mage was both experienced and powerful. Roman had met his type before. He was the kind of man who had very little respect for rank. He was looking at Wayne as if the head mercenary was some kind of middle manager making his job more difficult. Fulton liked to fuck shit up and get paid. He didn't like complications, he didn't have a lot of patience, and if you held his leash too tight, he would bite it off and leave. Wayne's face told Roman that Wayne knew all that.

"Finn," Wayne called out.

Uh huh. The reasonable tone was back.

"I get it. You're doing what a man is supposed to do. You made it through the woods, you didn't get caught. You found this place, and now you're trying to protect it and your new friend. I respect that. But sometimes no matter how hard you fight, you can't win, kid. Knowing that is part of growing up. A boy can be stubborn because he doesn't understand the consequences. A man must evaluate the situation and mitigate the damage."

Finn's shoulders slumped.

"Fulton here is in a bad mood because he marched all night and had to work hard when he got here."

Fulton rolled his eyes again.

"Don't let that fool you," Wayne said. "He's very good at what he does. His crew is one of the best. They have taken down people with a hell of a lot more power than you or the priest have. Once they get started, they will tear this whole place apart, and I won't be able to help you."

Well, at least he wasn't lying. Once Fulton got going, stopping him would require brute force. He gave off that thorough, scorched-earth vibe.

"I know you care what happens to these critters." Wayne dangled the melalo by his wing. "Or you wouldn't be out here on that porch. You've heard people say that a man has to do what a man has to do. Right now, you are that man. You can save everyone, Finn. All you have to do is go inside, grab your dog, and walk across this yard to us. That's all. Simple. Do that and nobody else dies today. I give you my word."

Finn swallowed. He seemed resigned.

"Take the deal, kid," Fulton said.

"I give up," Finn said.

Wayne shook his head. "Don't look at it that way. You're not giving up. You're doing the smart thing. The noble thing."

Something was brewing inside Finn. The shepherd puppy rose from her haunches and slunk to the front door.

Finn squeezed the staff. Klyuv's eyes bulged.

"Come on down." Wayne waved him over. "You can do this."

Finn opened his mouth. "Drop the melalo and set the antidote on the ground."

The two mercenaries stared at him.

"I don't want to write this big check."

Fulton looked at Wayne. "What the fuck is he talking about?"

"Who knows?"

"Do it now," Finn said.

"That's it," Fulton snapped. "Playtime is over. Now we're doing it my way."

"Remember, alive," Wayne said. "Him and the dog."

67

"On me!" Fulton stepped forward. "Arrowhead formation in three..."

Six soldiers stepped forward, taking positions behind Fulton in a rough triangle, like a flock of geese orienting behind the leader.

On the porch, Finn gripped the staff with both hands and planted it in front of him.

"...Two..."

The wall of the ward anchored to the nithing poles turned visible, a translucent barrier of pale silver. Fulton thrust his hands forward, and drew them apart, as if opening curtains. A gap formed directly in front of him.

A blinding white clump of magic accreted inside Finn, a storm pressurized into a tiny, hyper-dense point in his chest. The mercenaries didn't feel it behind their ward.

Fulton smiled. "...One."

Golden chains made of light snapped to Fulton from the six mages, funneling power into him. He opened his mouth, his eyes burning with magic. Flames sheathed his arms.

"*I accept,*" Finn whispered, his voice unnaturally loud. "*Help me, Morena!*"

The shepherd howled, her wail an eerie primal song filled with bloodlust.

The melalo clamped his beak onto Wayne's fingers. The mercenary flung him aside. The creature took off into the woods faster than Roman had ever seen him move before.

The blizzard inside Finn tore free. Ice shards stabbed out of the ground, crowding each other, charging toward the merce-naries like frozen waves. Cold gripped the yard, bitter, polar cold, as Winter herself exhaled. The Christmas tree snapped and splin-tered, its sap crystallized in an instant. Two birds plummeted from the sky, frozen in mid-flight.

The waves of ice slammed into the nithing poles and crunched, speeding up their shafts, turning the poles into six frozen popsicles. The runes winked out, extinguished. The ward tore, and seven people cried out in a chorus from the backlash. The mercenary mages stumbled back.

The biggest wave headed straight for Fulton.

A jet of flames erupted from the mage's hands, punching into the wall of ice rushing at him.

The ice kept coming.

Fulton screamed, his flames turning white. Steam burst from the impact of fire and ice.

The staff danced in Finn's hands. He grunted and pushed, struggling to put all he had into it, but he had nothing left.

The ice slid another two feet and stopped. Another half a foot, and Fulton would have lost his hands.

Finn slumped, hanging on to the staff to stay upright.

Fulton's flames died. He bent over in half, breathing heavily like he'd just sprinted 400 meters.

Wow. The kid packed a lot of power. Not much control but a lot of raw force. Roman smiled. Morena? would have her hands full with this one. Served her right.

The ice waves cracked and collapsed.

Fulton straightened. "Arrowhead on me!"

The six mages stepped forward like zombies rising from the dead.

"That was good, kid," Fulton called out. "I took you too lightly. But now you're done and I'm not. Not that you will get a chance to use it, but let me give you some advice. When it comes to magic, it's all about staying power."

Finn stared at him, rage burning in his eyes.

Fulton raised three fingers, then two. The golden chains shot to him again.

Finn stumbled. His body went one way, Klyuv went the other, and Roman stepped out onto the porch, catching both.

Finn gaped at him.

At the property line, Wayne swore.

Roman spat an incantation. Bone chains erupted from the ground, seizing Fulton and the six mages behind him into bone collars. Roman thrust his hand out, closed his fingers, and yanked. The chains dragged the struggling mercenaries into a clump, winding around them with Fulton in the center. Roman jerked them up, slammed them on the ground, jerked them up again, and hurled the whole mass of people and bones into the trees.

"How?" Finn sputtered. "You were dying."

"Funny thing about a god's tears—they pack a lot of divinity. Those assholes wish I was dying. Instead, I am pissed off and filled with the horrible love of my god. You did well, Finn. Come inside. It's time we talk about it."

ROMAN LEANED KLYUV AGAINST THE WALL AND PATTED THE STAFF. *Good boy.* Klyuv was picky about letting itself be touched. The kid still had all his fingers and both eyes, which was some kind of miracle.

"Go sit by the fire, Finn."

The kid stumbled off and landed on the floor in front of the fireplace like a sack of flour. He looked like death.

Roman tossed another chunk of wood into the fireplace, poked the logs with a stick to get them situated, and went to the kitchen. This called for heat and sugar. He pulled the bottle of sbiten out of the fridge. He'd made some three days ago, because he'd been craving it, but ended up just drinking his eggnog instead.

Eggnog would've so hit the spot right about now.

He poured sbiten into a kettle, returned to the living room, slid the kettle onto an iron hook attached to the fireplace, and swiveled the hook into the fire.

Finn sat unmoving. The shepherd puppy had wedged herself

next to him, her head on his lap, and was looking at him with devoted eyes.

The doggie door banged. A moment later the melalo scurried into the living room and hid behind the metal ash bucket, half of his good head with a small, round eye sticking out.

"There you are, paskudnik."

The melalo shivered.

"Look at what you've wrought. Got yourself caught, now the child is traumatized."

"It wasn't his fault," Finn muttered. "They were trying to catch Fedya. He ran at them to distract them."

"Is that true?"

The melalo shivered again. Roman got up, came back with a piece of jerky, and held it out. The melalo scooted from behind the bucket, snagged the jerky, and ran back to his hiding spot.

Steam escaped the kettle's spout. Hot enough. Roman pulled the swivel arm out of the fire with the fire poker, grabbed the kettle's handle with a folded towel, and poured two mugs of the hot brew. The scent of spices filled the room. He handed one mug to Finn. "Drink."

"What is it?"

"Sbiten. Honey, jam, water, and spices. Will warm you right up."

Finn sipped. Some color came back into his face.

Roman landed in his favorite spot on the couch and drank from his mug. "I'm all ears."

Finn looked into his mug.

"We're past the point where you can be shy about it," Roman told him.

"They took my sister."

"Who?"

Finn gave him a dark look. "The gods."

"The Slavic gods?"

He nodded. "She made some kind of deal with them. She is

71

always off, doing something they want. Sometimes she comes home, but she never stays longer than a couple of days."

Not unusual. Deals with gods always came with strings attached. The question was, what did his sister get out of that deal?

"Then, last year, in February, I started getting these dreams. Winter, northern lights. Snow. Ice. Dark forest." Finn drank more sbiten. "I would wake up and the bed would be covered in frost."

That sounded about right.

"Did you have powers before that?"

Finn shook his head.

"This happened before with my sister, but in a different way. My parents took me to Biohazard. There is a man there who can tell what your magic is."

"Luther Dillon."

Finn glanced up. "You know him?"

Roman nodded. Luther was a rarity—a powerful, formally educated mage who didn't have his head up his ass.

"What did Luther say?"

Finn's eyes turned dark. "He said I was chosen by a pagan god. He couldn't tell which one, so he narrowed it down to two: Ullr and Morena. When he said her name, it was like a bell rang in my head."

Better than pain.

"I looked up what she is," Finn said. "She is evil, cold, and dark. She's the goddess of death and winter. There was a family in New York that offended her, and she froze all of them, even the babies."

"She did. It wasn't just a family, it was Lihoradka's cult, and they incubated a plague inside themselves, but yes, she did freeze them all. Even the babies. Subtlety isn't what gods are good at. That's why they have us. We mitigate."

"Well, I don't want to worship her. I'm not even Slavic. None of our family is. She shouldn't have picked me."

"You don't have to be Slavic for a Slavic god to pick you. My neighbor is Polish. Not a Celtic bone in his body. But druidism spoke to him, and so he is a druid."

"Well, at least he had a choice!"

The sbiten was clearly doing its job. The kid had come back to life.

"And you didn't?"

"It didn't feel like it. She left me alone during this last summer, but in September it started again. Snow, blood, cold, every night. I'd wake up, and my windows would be frozen. The pipes in my bathroom burst twice. It cost a lot of money to fix." Finn slumped. "She hounded me."

"They do that." Roman took a swallow of his drink. "Speaking of hounds, when did the dog show up?"

"A month ago. I found her shivering in the rain by our porch." He petted the puppy, and she licked his hand. "I didn't know Athena was a special dog. I only found out three days ago."

"You named Morena's sacred animal after a Greek goddess?" Roman sighed.

Finn's jawline hardened.

"I get it," Roman said. "An occasional screw-up is allowed. Just remember you have to earn it. What happened three days ago?"

"I had a nightmare."

It must've shaken him. His eyes turned haunted.

"What did you see?"

"My parents. They were dead in our house," Finn said quietly.

Heavy. "Anything else?"

"A priest in front of an altar. He had Athena on it. He cut her throat with a long, curved knife. Her blood was all over the altar, and it was glowing with green and purple lights. It felt...real."

The shepherd whined softly. Finn petted her again.

"What happened next?"

"Her blood froze, and I heard a woman's voice. She said that if I wanted to keep my parents, my dog, and myself alive, I had to run. She said to follow the dog, and when I got to the fir tree in front of a big house, ask for sanctuary, and stay there until my sister came. Then she told me to wake up, and I did. I got dressed, took my backpack and Athena, and left."

Mystery solved. Morena must've been really convincing. Probably scared him out of his mind. Didn't clarify why those assholes outside were hunting him though.

"I'm sorry," Finn said.

"For what?"

"For coming here. You got hurt because of me."

Roman shrugged. "All part of the job. I have to say, that's the first time someone asked me for sanctuary, but turns out, I'm rather good at providing it. Catholics, eat your heart out."

"You joke a lot," Finn said.

"I do. Helps with the darkness."

"Why do you do it? Why do you serve Chernobog?"

And here we go. "Usually, I quip something witty here about it being a family business or that I love the dark power. But I'm going to give you the real answer, as a professional courtesy. I do it, because someone has to, Finn. Like it or not, gods exist. Even the weakest of them have enough power to ruin lives and bring unimaginable misery to our world. We serve as intermediaries between them and the rest of humanity. We guard the boundary."

Finn stared at him.

"It's a shit job no matter what god you serve. People don't seek divine intervention because their lives are going well. They come to you when they are desperate. When a child has been taken, when the crops have failed, when plague is burning through their loved ones, when nothing else has helped. They come ridden with guilt and filled with pain. And your job is to listen to their tragedies, take it all in, offer kindness and understanding, and then go to your god and beg them for salvation and mercy. Sometimes it's granted. Sometimes you bargain for hours, and you get them from fifty righteous men to ten, and then you can't find the damn ten righteous men, and the entire city gets destroyed, and you carry that with you for the rest of your life, but at least you tried. It takes a particular person to do this. You don't get a thank you often. There will be times when you will try your best, and people you've bled and fought for will spit on you and curse your name. But it's a job that must be done."

Finn looked away. "What if I can't do it?"

"Do you know why Morena wants you? Yes, it's because of your magic and compatibility, but also because you don't want the job. You will not abuse it. I've had a front row seat to what happens when a priest is seduced by the power. It's not pretty. You won't be one of those. I can tell. You can say no, Finn. Even though you've invoked, you can still renounce Morena and quit. The choice is yours."

The house fell silent, except for the cracking of the logs in the fireplace and the soothing purr of the korgorusha watching them with glowing eyes.

"If I do this, will anyone even come to me?" Finn said quietly. "Would they even ask for my help?"

"Of course they will. Why wouldn't they?"

"Pagans kill Morena every spring. They make an effigy out of straw, and they throw it in the river."

Roman nodded. "True."

"They *drown* her. Every year."

"Sometimes they also burn her."

"People hate her that much."

He almost laughed, but held it in. Pragmatism came with age and exposure, and the boy had neither.

"Hate is a strong word here. People do fear Morena. They are cautious with her name. They don't implore her unless shit has truly hit the fan. But that doesn't mean they hate her or that they don't want her blessing."

Finn looked skeptical.

"One thing you learn when you become a priest, once the shock and awe wears off, is that most things are simpler than you imagined them to be. The traditions and rituals we perform aren't just for the gods. They are for us, for humans. In a way, it's fan service."

"What?"

"The drowning ritual—the correct word for us, Slavic pagans, is obryad—takes place at the beginning of spring. The weather is nice, the skies are blue, and you don't have to wrap a scarf over your face to keep your nose from freezing off. After being cooped up all winter, you can dress up in something that has some shape to it, get together with other people your age, decorate a dolly with branches and ribbons, and toss it into the water or set it on fire."

Finn frowned.

Roman smiled at him. "You know who loves this holiday? Teenagers like you. They come out in droves to check each other out and flirt. Morena started out as an agrarian goddess. Not exactly the same, but similar roots as the Assyrian Ishtar and Greek Demeter. Common theme for their spring rites? Fertility."

Finn blinked.

"See, you've built this whole tragedy around 'people are murdering my goddess' when in reality it's all about celebrating surviving the winter by shopping for a date. I've asked Morena before how she felt about it."

"You did?"

"I did. You know what she said? 'Finally, vacation time.'" Roman drained the last of his sbiten and set the mug aside. "Now let's take a look at that nightmare of yours."

[6]

"Water is the boundary between worlds." Roman placed a heavy glass dish onto the table. "It holds magic like nothing else. It can hide you. It can kill you. Water is your element. Why?"

"Snow and ice?" Finn guessed.

Roman nodded. "Exactly. Go out back and bring me a small icicle."

The kid took off. Roman filled the bowl to about an inch from the rim and retrieved a small mirror, paper, and a pen from his office.

Finn came back with a small icicle.

"Sit."

Finn sat at the table.

Roman took a piece of paper and drew a cross set on its side, two intersecting lines connecting the square's corners. He crossed each corner with a smaller line and showed it to Finn.

"Morena's znak."

"Znek?"

"*Znuck*. Rhymes with *puck*. Means symbol. That's your goddess's sigil." Roman held up the mirror.

"It's a stylized snowflake. Except snowflakes have six sides."

"This one has four. Ancient Slavs didn't know about hydrogen bonds or hexagonal lattice. Morena pauses flowing water. Her sigil stands for halting, keeping still, stopping in its tracks. It's a powerful ward. We are going to use it to freeze-frame a memory. Use the icicle to draw it on your forehead. Doesn't need to be precise. Just do the best you can."

Finn scribbled with the icicle on his forehead.

"Drop it into the bowl."

The icicle landed in the water.

"Repeat after me. 'Mother Morena, light of winter...'"

"'...light of winter...'"

"'Life- preserving, snow-bringing, guardian of seeds, keeper of roots...'"

"'...roots...'"

"'Peer into my mind and bring forth a memory.'"

"'...memory.'"

"'Let me see the face of my enemy.'"

"'...enemy.'"

"Look into the bowl and think back to your nightmare."

Finn stared at the water.

Magic moved. A thin layer of ice sheathed the surface, clear like glass. Within it, an image formed like a photograph appearing in a Polaroid. A tall man in a complex garment standing in front of a plain stone altar. Behind him, a symbol glowed, a wheel with eight spokes, drawn in the air with thin, smoldering lines, like glowing wires burning against wood.

Six spokes ended in sharp triangles; another, at seven-thirty o'clock, was severed in half; and the top one, pointing straight up, split in two just before it reached the outer rim.

Three rings, the smallest inner ring at about one-quarter of the radius, and then an outer, double ring. So three and then multiples of two, specifically four and eight. Those were these people's sacred numbers.

A dark gray robe with bright yellow panels, not cinched or belted, but cut narrow at the waist; long gray sleeves, close-fitted; dark gray gloves; two thick cords hanging from the shoulders, caught with metal clamps and ending in long tassels; and over it, a bright yellow cloak or over-robe, draping over the shoulders and arms, over the top part of the chest, and forming a layered hood. Beautiful fabric, embroidered with complex patterns, almost brocade-like, but not nearly as heavy, judging by the drape. The edges of the hood and the hem of the robe were tattered and fraying.

Roman had never seen anything like this before. The cut of the robe was definitely martial, more battle monk than ceremonial clergy. None of the symbology on the fabric rang any bells.

The deep hood hid most of the priest's face, leaving only the bottom half of his face exposed. Olive complexion, short, dark beard. That told him exactly nothing.

The priest held a long knife in his gloved hand, curved like a talon, with the same wheel symbol etched on the blade.

That was it.

The wheel didn't look like it was from any religion Roman knew, but there was something vaguely familiar about it. It invited comparison with the dharmachakra, the wheel of dharma. Hinduism, Buddhism, and Jainism all used it. In Hinduism, it was associated with the sun, light, and knowledge. In Buddhism, it represented Buddha's teachings. The dharmachakra was an auspicious sign. This wheel was anything but. It didn't look right.

It didn't feel right, either. The glowing symbol felt oppressive, a weapon such as a buzz saw blade rather than a chariot wheel.

He had seen it somewhere before, but where?

"Did the priest say anything in your dream?" he asked.

"No."

"Did you hear any voices, anything at all besides Morena?"

"No."

"Alright. You can let it go."

Finn relaxed and the ice melted, taking the image with it. "What now?"

"Now we dig deeper."

"How? Another obryad?"

"No. We're going to make coffee and then we're going into my office, where we will look through a bunch of old books until we find something that fits."

Finn blinked.

"It's not all blood and flashy magic. A lot of it is scholarship. Get used to it."

"I SEE WHAT YOU MEAN ABOUT THE DHARMIC WHEEL." THE TINY brown-headed nuthatch hopped back and forth, studying the drawing. "Harmony and symmetry are the point, and this is nothing like that. It's not a chariot wheel."

"No, if it were a chariot wheel, there would have been a solid circle to denote the axle, but the spokes intersect in the center."

"Exactly. It's not a nautical wheel, either. It's something vicious."

Roman rubbed his face. In the chair by the window, Finn stared at the massive tome in his lap, his eyes glazed over. The shepherd puppy had fallen asleep by his feet.

After the mercenaries collected the mage squad he'd hurled into the woods, they had dug in and gone quiet. A couple of hours ago Fedya, the smallest koloversh, brought an update: the client was coming in person.

They needed to figure out what they were dealing with before that client arrived. Forewarned was forearmed. Except he and Finn had been at this for hours now and had come up with nothing. He'd sent a koloversh to Dabrowski as a last resort.

"But does it look familiar to you?" Roman asked.

"That's the damnedest thing," Dabrowski said through the

bird. "It does. Either I've seen it before or read about it. Otherworld alone knows where or when. Your apprentice is wilting."

Roman glanced at Finn.

The kid sighed. "Do we really have to know all of this?"

"Yes," Roman and Dabrowski said at the same time.

"But these are other people's gods."

"And if we were living in a world with just one god, it wouldn't be an issue," Dabrowski said.

"We would have much bigger issues," Roman said.

"True," the druid agreed.

"You won't be serving *the* God, Finn. You will be serving *a* god," Roman said. "The problem with clergy is that we don't just minister, we seek to convert, and many of us view other religions as rivals."

The nuthatch hopped around. "Indeed. Lock five priests from different cults into the same room for an hour, and at the end you have an equal chance of either harmony or a theological bloodbath. You won't know which it is until you open that door. It's like the Schrödinger Synod. Although *synod* isn't exactly the best term..."

Roman had to cut him off before Dabrowski veered off on a tangent.

"The point is, you need to know who you are dealing with and what they are capable of. And religions grow and evolve all the time, so you must keep up. Druids like Piotr here can be monotheists, duotheists, or polytheists. Some reject the concept of a deity altogether, and yet when they gather, they have no problem performing the same rites and rituals, and all of them follow the same fundamental ethics. Chop an oak sapling in front of them and see how united they will get."

"Why?" Finn asked.

"Because Druidry is both a religion and a way of life," Dabrowski said. "It is a path, a journey, measured in time rather than distance, which all of us undertake together. Life is fundamentally spiritual, nature is unknowable, and none of us have a monopoly on the truth."

"But what do you believe?" Finn asked.

"I believe that—"

The dog door flap thudded, and a huge raven flew into the office and landed on Roman's desk.

Damn it all.

"There you are," the raven said in his mother's voice.

The nuthatch cringed. "Hello, Mrs. Tihomirov."

"Petya. And what are you doing here?"

"Leaving, actually." Dabrowski hopped off the table and flew off into the house.

Coward.

Roman sighed. "Yes?"

"Yes? That's all you have to say to me?"

Chernobog, grant me patience...

"I know this is a hard time of the year for you. The whole family is at the house celebrating and you are stuck out here alone like some frozen mushroom. I made your favorite pirogi. I kept waiting and waiting to see if you would reach out. I didn't want to smother you."

The Void is darkness, the Void is peace, I am within it, wrapped in its cold embrace, and I am at peace...

"You do not call. You do not answer. Is your phone broken? No? You probably unplugged it again. You do not send a word with one of your critters. For three days I have waited."

Nothing reaches the Void for it is the beginning and end of all things...

"Finally, I come to check on you and find you surrounded by some zarazas who try to shoot my bird, you look like death warmed over, and all you can say to me is, 'yes'?"

Within the Void I am serene.

"What an ungrateful son I have. Why haven't you killed them yet? What have you been doing?"

Chernobog, grant me patience.

"As you can see, I have company." Roman glanced at Finn. "This is Finn, Morena's new priest. Finn, this is my mother, Evdokia, the Head Witch of the Witch Oracle."

The raven pivoted to Finn, who stared back like a deer in headlights.

"Finn is my guest. The dickheads outside are soldiers-for-hire, and they've been hired by their client to apprehend Finn. If I kill them, that wouldn't solve the problem, would it? It would just postpone it because we don't know who the client is, and they will try again."

The raven peered at Finn.

A few seconds passed.

A few more.

"Ha!" The raven cackled. "Karma!"

"What?"

"That's the consequence of your own actions sitting in that chair. And this one was a long time coming."

Roman stared at Finn. No, there was no way. "He isn't mine."

"Would that he was! If he were your child, that would be a miracle. One I would joyously welcome. If you managed to sire a son, I would strip naked and run around the woods like one of those Beltane nudists."

Roman squeezed his eyes shut before his brain had a chance to grapple with that mental image. "Mother!"

"What is wrong with you? You are thirty-four years old. I can see gray hair on your head. How is it you haven't made any babies yet?"

Void...

"Have you had yourself checked?"

"For what?" he snarled.

"For low sperm count."

Roman groaned.

"How is your testosterone? Or is that you are having trouble sealing the deal? If you're having equipment malfunctions, I have herbs for that—"

"Mother!" he roared.

"And now you are yelling at me. Because why not, go ahead, yell at your mother, who was in labor with you for two days."

"Every year the labor gets longer. Maybe your memory isn't what it used to be."

The raven fell ominously silent. Oh shit.

"It's been twelve years, sweetheart," Mother said, sadness filling her voice.

Oh, Nav no.

"Every year you and I reenact this play, where I come and nag so you know we care, and every year you run away and refuse to talk about it. Let it go. Nobody blames you. Nobody ever blamed you, for it was never your fault. It's time to rejoin the living, don't you think? Find someone to love. Stop punishing yourself and let yourself breathe a bit. We miss you. Your father—"

Anything but that talk. Not again. He grabbed the drawing of the wheel and thrust it in front of the raven. "What does that look like to you?"

The raven sighed and studied the drawing. "Some New Age otsebyachenna. It's not even symmetrical."

"Do you think Dad might know?"

"Your father is into his third cup of medovuha. He told me he loved me a few minutes ago, so I wouldn't count on it."

The raven pivoted to Finn again. "Is your sister coming?"

"Yes," Finn said.

"Good." The raven turned to Roman. "Life comes full circle, son. If only I was here to see it. Unfortunately, your own sister just walked through the door, so I must go. Deal with your mess and come down to see your family. Bring your guests, too."

The awareness died in the raven's eyes. It sat there for another moment confused, shook its feathers, and flew out the back door.

Full circle. Now why did that ring a bell…?

Something stirred in his head. Some weak fragment of a memory.

"What's otsebyachenna?" Finn asked.

"Made-up nonsense. Something you came up with yourself without any foundation or research."

Full circle...

The flock of kolovershi rushed into the room, followed by the iron hound.

"What is it?"

Something sparked on the edge of his awareness, a jagged, nasty kind of magic like lightning woven of razor blades. They had run out of time.

Roman rose. "The client is here."

Two people stood at the boundary of the property. Both wore garments of gray and bright egg-yolk-yellow. Finn's nightmare had come to life.

Roman reached for his binoculars.

The one on the left sported a layered robe with the familiar hood and yellow over-robe. The hood was up. The face within it was solid gray, painted with some sort of pigment. A narrow vertical stripe of bright yellow bisected it, running down the forehead, over the bridge of the nose, and over the lips and the chin. Impossible to say if it was a man or a woman, young or old.

A dead ringer for the asshole in the dream, although the yellow fabric was much less luxurious, and the hems of their robes and hood had just begun to fray. Probably the younger model of the other priest, still doing fieldwork.

The priest carried two weapons: the same curved knife Finn saw in his vision and a weird-looking axe that hung on their left hip, with a shaft made from a twisted tree limb. The axe handle was wrapped in a braided cord and terminated in a narrow, brutal axe-head, less a blade and more a wide spike.

The person next to the priest was taller, with broad shoulders, their garment layered, but fitted tighter and cut simpler, more a knight's tabard than a priest's robe, caught just above the hips by a plain black belt. An ornate black scabbard hung from the belt, holding a sword with a black handle. Their cloak was plain and gray, and a long, yellow sash dripped from underneath, its edges tattered. A gray half-mask guarded the face within the hood. The eyes above the mask were dark and cold under thick, brown eyebrows.

A priest and a knight. Magic and melee, both covered.

Behind the odd pair, Wayne and Fulton waited, looking unsure. Fulton leaned on a makeshift cane made from a freshly cut sapling. The flight through the woods must've ended in a rough landing. Heh. Wayne had developed some weird-looking bumps on his face. They seemed to be oozing pus. What do you know, the little bird still packed a punch even with one head.

"The priest has the same knife as in my dream," Finn said.

"And what does that tell you?"

"The knife is ceremonial. It's used in sacrifices. They have the kind of religion that makes their priests carry sacrificial knifes all the time."

Smart kid. Morena had chosen well.

Wayne opened his mouth.

Roman focused, pulling the sound to himself.

"So, like I was saying," Wayne explained, "The boy is inside, and the priest took out half of my team."

The gray and yellow duo showed no indication of having heard or cared.

"He is packing serious power," Fulton said. "I wouldn't recommend going in there balls to the wall."

The knight unsheathed their sword. A straight double-edged affair, about three feet overall with a thirty-inch blade. Good for cutting and thrusting.

Here we go. "Finn, go to the back room where the fridge is.

Turn left. There is a box sitting on the second shelf, looks like a pirate chest. Bring it to me."

Finn took off running.

Behind the knight, the priest raised their hands. Magic snapped between their fingertips, an invisible, jagged line of power. The priest stretched it, shaping it, their movements practiced and complex, almost hypnotic, a blend of martial and ritual.

"What's the plan?" Fulton demanded. "Do you want us to back you up? Do you need auxiliary support?"

The magic gained color. It wasn't a glow or a radiance. No, it was viscous, a kind of ichor or plasma stretching between the priest's hands, a bright, shocking yellow that smudged and hung in the air. It felt like nothing Roman had experienced. Divine and yet not divine, filtered through human magic, but not limited to it. Alien. Unnatural.

What the actual fuck…

The knight spun in place, twisting and turning, their hands snapping into well-practiced forms. Yellow plasma sheathed the knight's sword.

Finn rounded the corner, slid across the floor, and thrust the chest at him.

They would need to be outside for this. Roman swiped Klyuv from its spot against the wall, stuck the staff into his armpit, and took the chest. The front door swung open in front of him on its own. Roman stepped onto the porch, sending a spike of power through each foot as it touched the floorboards. The skulls on the posts burst into blue fire, rattling their jaws.

The knight and priest paused.

Now you know what you're dealing with. Walk away and live.

The priest twisted, spinning their yellow ichor. The knight started forward, slow, deliberate, unhurried.

It's like that then? Fine.

Roman set his staff down, planting Klyuv into the porch boards. The staff remained upright, held by magic. Klyuv's vicious eyes rotated in their orbits. The wicked beak gaped in a silent scream and clacked closed, crushing imaginary bones. Darkness poured out of the spot where the staff met the floor, spreading along the ground, blanketing the front yard in a foot of evil fog.

The knight took two more steps, untroubled. The darkness swirled around them, clinging to their boots and pants.

A ring of yellow plasma formed behind the priest, eight feet tall, and it hung there like a wagon wheel with the familiar irregular spoke arrangement.

Roman flicked his left hand. A giant bone hand erupted from the ground and backhanded the knight. The warrior flew backward a few yards, flipped in the air, and landed on their feet just outside of the boundary. The mask cracked and fell off, revealing a man in his late twenties.

Nice acrobatics.

Roman opened the chest. Black soil waited inside. He dipped his fingers into it, scooping a handful. It was soft like powder, slightly moist, and cold to the touch. Its magic licked his skin, cold, ancient, terrible, unknowable, and unfeeling, the magic that was there before humans and would be there after they passed.

Finn recoiled. "What is that?"

"Soil from the border between Nav and the Void. Whatever you do, do not step off the porch."

Roman barked an incantation, snapping each word, and tossed the handful of Nav dirt into his yard. It sank into the fog, and he felt it burrow into the ground. Otherworldly magic spread through the ground, sliding just under the surface, awakening things he'd buried years ago. He could feel it rush through his yard, widening in a ring around his house, a magic field just under the fog.

Across the yard, the priest crossed their arms and threw them to the sides, as if cutting an invisible enemy with their hands. The yellow wheel behind the priest rotated toward the house, launching gobs of ichor that stretched and snapped into slender swords in midair.

Roman jerked his arm up. The bone hands burst out of the ground in front of the porch, shielding them from the yellow barrage. The giant fingers shuddered under the bombardment. Bone splinters rained onto the porch.

The magic Gatling gun kept firing.

"Should I...?" Finn offered.

"No."

The kid packed a truckload of power, but without training, he used it on pure instinct. When he unleashed his magic, he would do exactly what he'd done before—he'd sink it all into one terrifying burst and then he would be tapped out. They had to save it for the right moment.

Chunks of bone pelted the ground. The yellow blades kept coming, slicing into the bone shield with a hiss. The left ring finger broke, then the right index finger, falling to the ground. Roman could see the lawn through the gaps, and the flashes of yellow around the attackers.

Fuckers. It would take a lot of bone to regrow the hands.

Ancient magic shifted underneath the fog. Almost there.

The glow of the knight's sword split into eight lines, like thin ribbons emanating from the blade. They wrapped around the knight. He charged, unnaturally fast, covering ten yards in a blink.

The moment his foot touched inside the magic field, the lawn yawned underneath him. It was as if the solid ground itself had sprouted a mouth and opened wide, its edges studded with razor-sharp bone teeth. The Void hungered for life and magic. It would devour anything it touched.

The warrior leaped up, drawing a circle with his sword as he twisted in the air. The earth jaws followed him like a great white shark breaching and gulped him down.

The left bone hand shattered. A glowing sword shot through the gap. Roman yanked Finn out of the way, and the blade sank into the front door, which melted into a blob of magic that sizzled like acid.

Roman bared his teeth.

Two knots of magic coalesced just under the surface of the soil and sped toward the priest, leaving trails in the fog.

The priest continued twisting their arms, oblivious, focused on their spellcasting.

The ground in front of the priest crested in twin waves, fanged mouths sliding within it.

The priest jumped straight up. Simultaneously the wheel fell forward, and the priest passed through its center. The wheel spun, its edge chewing at the ravenous dirt. Above it, the priest hovered in midair, waving their arms, throwing the yellow plasma back and forth in a complex frenzy.

And they could fly. Great, just great. What's next? Fire-spitting?

The mass of soil that had swallowed the warrior burst. He sprung free, swinging his sword in a wide arc, no worse for wear. Shit.

"That's not good, right?" Finn asked.

"It's not great, kid."

The priest jerked the knife from their belt and stabbed it downward in a wide arc. The yellow ichor flew off the blade and bit into the ground. A phantom mouth sank red-hot teeth into Roman's stomach and tore out a chunk of flesh. The pain was raw and hot, and it took all of his will not to clamp his hand over his actual gut to check himself.

An eight-foot-wide chunk of the magic field vanished from Roman's mental horizon, its edges burning with pain. A hole had formed in the fog, revealing a circle of bare ground. Thin yellow tendrils sprouted from it, like the tentacles of some upside-down jellyfish. The wheel slid forward over them, carrying the priest with it.

The priest stabbed the ground to their right. Agony blossomed in Roman. Another chunk of the fog vanished, more tentacles slivered out, and the warrior moved onto them and ran across the thin tendrils as if they were solid ground, leaping in front of the priest onto the rim of the wheel. It was still spinning, and he should've fallen off, except his feet didn't touch the edge. He hovered six inches above the glowing yellow monstrosity and clamped his hands together. Thin red vapor emanated from his body, flowing upward and turning bright yellow.

"What's happening?" Finn demanded.

"They're feeding on my consecrated ground. Consuming the magic to fuel whatever the hell that yellow shit is."

Throwing more dirt at them would do nothing. It would just give them more magic to eat. He had to bring down the priest and the wheel. It was the only way.

Roman swung his hand, clawing at the air. Dark missiles tore out of the fog and streaked toward the priest.

The warrior shifted his stance. The line of yellow above him snapped into an eight-foot-tall sword dripping with magic. The sword sliced through the clumps of darkness, sucking them in. The missiles vanished.

Fuck.

The priest spun around and stabbed again. Pain, hole, the wheel sliding forward.

They were in deep shit.

There was always the other option.

No, anything but that. What was the point of making grand pronouncements if one didn't follow through? He had his pride. He'd meant what he said—he was done. He had gotten this far on his power alone, and he wasn't tapped out yet. There were still things he could do.

He began chanting low under his breath.

Magic appeared at the end of the driveway, so bright, so potent, so radiant, that for a second, he faltered.

The pair on the wheel felt it too. The warrior slipped to the side, trying to keep Roman and the newcomer in his view.

A cloaked figure strode toward his house.

The mercenaries pivoted toward it.

He knew this magic. It felt so achingly familiar, so right, like coming home after a long, terrible journey and finding the fire lit and the table set. It hugged him, and he had to fight the urge to step off the porch toward it.

The figure lowered their hood. A woman. A lovely woman with dark blond hair put away into a braid.

"That's my sister!"

Sister... *Gods took her away...* The pieces fell into place. "Your sister is a Vasylisa?"

"Yes. Is that important?"

Damn it, Finn.

As long as Slavic neopagans existed, there would always be a Vasylisa. She was the heroine of countless folkloric tales, a woman with magic and secret knowledge, blessed by the pagan gods. Princes fought over her, dragons and evil undead kidnapped her, wandering heroes battled her for the privilege of her hand and the keys to her domain. She was the frog princess, the Amazon warrior, the guardian of the fire bird and the golden apples.

The first one showed up shortly after the Shift. When she was killed, another one manifested the powers and took her place. There had been several since, always one at a time. He'd met the previous Vasylisa years ago, and the meeting had been seared into his memory.

In the pantheon of Light and Dark, Vasylisas walked on the border, choosing their own path, an expression of female power and knowledge, heirs to both witches and warriors. They settled disputes when Slavic gods got in a tiff, they acted on prophecies to prevent disasters, and removed threats to the cosmic equilibrium. Some were stronger, others were weaker, but none should be taken lightly.

And they came in two varieties, Prekrasnaya and Premudraya. The Beautiful and the Wise. The first one was enchanting, alluring, and irresistible, relying on magical charm and manipulation to make armies kneel and entice powerful people to do her bidding. The second was a creature of deep magic, a sorceress with offensive powers, unpredictable and sharp.

And looking at her now, Roman had no idea which she was.

"Is she the Beautiful or the Wise?"

Finn made a face. "She's my sister!"

Damn it. Roman resumed his chant.

The Vasylisa didn't even look at the two mercenaries. Her voice was cold. "Leave."

"What the fuck..." Wayne sounded resigned. Clearly, the man was at his limit for weird magical shit happening. "Who the fuck are you, lady? What are you doing here?"

The Vasylisa looked past them, straight at Roman. Their stares connected. He was full-on chanting now, building his magic into an intricate net and twisting it like a rubber band. She looked at him like they had met before, but for the life of him, he couldn't imagine why. He would have remembered *her*. Absolutely.

Please be the Wise, please be the Wise...

"Look here," Fulton started. "I've had just about enough of this bullshit. I'm a level III pyro. I don't know what—"

The Vasylisa unsheathed a sword. It had a double-edged blade about thirty inches long, with a wide, shallow fuller and a simple copper cross guard. It looked like something that came out of the Kievan Rus' burial grounds, an artifact from 1,200 years ago when the Varangian army of Viking mercenaries clashed with the Khazars over control of the fertile Eurasian plains.

The priest whirled. Long strands of yellow ichor stretched upward from the wheel's rim. The wheel spun faster, and the strands of yellow spiraled up, forming a protective lattice around the wheel.

The Vasylisa's sword burst into white flames.

Fulton gaped at the sword, grabbed Wayne by the arm, and yanked the mercenary leader aside, out of the way.

She was still looking directly at Roman, and he read an unspoken communication in her gaze.

Hit them at the same time.

The last tendril of Roman's magic slid into place.

He opened his mouth.

The Vasylisa raised her sword.

Roman spoke the last word of the incantation, sinking his magic into it. "*...pogibi!*"

Perish!

The curse tore out of him, a line of deep darkness vibrating with flashes of purple, streaking forward like a serpent's tongue. His magic, his raw human power, shaped by his will into a weapon.

The Vasylisa also struck. Blinding fire slid off her sword, cut across the ground, and tore into the dead center of the wheel. It cleaved through the yellow lattice. The ichor met the white fire and sizzled, burning into nothing. The rim of the wheel split with a magic crack. It careened and crashed.

The warrior leapt off a fraction of a moment before the slash had hit, but the priest missed their chance by half a second. Roman's dark lightning bit into them, jerking the pair into the air. The priest convulsed, screaming in a high-pitched voice. The yellow tendrils vanished. The wheel melted into nothing.

The warrior dashed toward the Vasylisa. She met him head on. They clashed, pale fire and yellow ichor flying.

The priest twisted in the air, still twisted by spasms. With a sharp jerk they yanked their dagger from its sheath.

"No, you bastard!" Roman roared.

The priest stabbed themselves in the heart.

Magic geysered out of their body, a torrent of lifeforce, blood, and power, all surrendered in an ancient, forbidden bargain. The torrent broke into a yellow fog, swallowing the priest. A deafening rumble filled the air, like the sound of an approaching tornado.

"What's happening?!" Finn yelled.

"The asshole sacrificed themselves! Something is coming!"

The blast of noise vanished, abruptly cut off. Thunder pealed. The yellow fog winked out of existence.

A colossal figure towered above the lawn. A beast, a horrible zoological fractal of terrifying body parts: snapping turtle jaws, crocodile teeth, six narrow, yellow eyes glowing with mad fire, a body twisted together with muscle, sinew, bone, and chitin into a semblance of a lion or maybe an ape... There were no words in Roman's vocabulary to adequately describe it.

It opened its mouth. Gobs of yellow ichor fell onto the trees, and yellow tendrils spiraled out from the splatter, choking the pines. A bellow rolled out. The wave of alien magic hit Roman. He thrust Klyuv out and braced, gripping Finn by the shoulder.

It was like trying to hold back a raging river. Instantly, he knew that nothing in his arsenal would touch it. He was almost spent. It took all of his remaining power to shield them from its roar.

At the other end of the lawn, the Vasylisa screamed, her voice completely silent, drowned out by the wall of sound. Fulton's mages had linked their arms into a circle around the rest of the mercenaries, trying to protect them with their combined power. One of Wayne's snipers, caught outside of the circle, made a desperate break for it but exploded from the inside out in mid-step, drenching the snow with gore.

The beast shut its mouth, looking around.

Roman had no choice. He would have to swallow his pride or everyone around them would die. This thing would kill Finn, the Vasylisa, him, the mercenaries, and then it would move on to Dabrowski and Schatten, and then to the outskirts of the city.

He had to buy time to bargain.

"Finn, ask Morena for the wail!"

The kid blinked. "What would a whale do? There is no water!"

"For fuck's sake, kid! Don't you know anything? The scream! Ask her for her scream!"

Finn looked up, whispering.

The colossus shifted its weight. The ground trembled. It hadn't even taken a step yet.

Finn's eyes rolled back into his head. His mouth opened.

An unearthly wail ripped from Finn's mouth, a raw, overpowering sound of pure anguish, the cry of a goddess abandoned, tormented, and betrayed by her family. The sheer potency of it was stupefying. It hit the colossus, and the creature staggered back, stunned for a few moments.

Roman shut his eyes, seeking the familiar darkness.

A figure loomed before him, his presence more than any human could endure.

I need help.

Silence.

If you don't help me, the boy will perish. She will be angrier.

An image of the fir tree abandoned in the snow appeared before him.

Yes, fine, I will drag the tree.

The unfathomable power that was Chernobog reached out and touched him.

Roman was back on the porch. Power filled him, spreading from him like a dark mantle. It coalesced, and he felt the familiar weight of Chernobog's spiked crown on his brow.

Finn, who had doubled over, jerked up straight with a startled gasp.

Roman was Darkness, eternal and ever-changing. The end of all things. The Final Cold.

The beast sighted him. It took one massive step forward.

The words dropped from Roman's lips:

"CHERNOBOSHE, LORD OF NAV, MY GOD, AID ME IN MY HOUR OF NEED."

A black bow appeared in his hands. He drew it, and a black arrow formed in his fingers, sizzling with power.

Roman fired.

The arrow sliced into the creature, ridiculously small, a needle piercing a giant.

There were few absolute truths in the universe, and yet one of them always endured, for it was woven into the very existence of reality: change was constant. From the moment the Universe was Born, it began to Decay. And Chernobog was the personification of that Decay.

The arrow sank into the creature. A brown stain spread from the wound.

The beast jerked and fell apart, collapsing into gobs of putrid flesh. Chunks of its body rained down, disintegrating into dust as they fell. Another moment, and there was nothing left. Only the empty yard.

At the mouth of the driveway, the Vasylisa cut the warrior's head off his shoulders. It bounced and rolled to her feet.

The mercenaries fled. This was no structured retreat; no, they turned and ran, a pack of panicked human animals fleeing for their lives, down the driveway and out of sight.

Everything was still.

Roman let go of the bow. It hung in the empty air for a moment and then dissipated like the fragments of a nightmare.

The Vasylisa stepped over the dead warrior's head and strode to the porch. He watched her come. Her magic was a muted light, hidden now, drawn inward. She was in her late twenties, half a foot shorter than him, and moved lightly on her feet. She was like a snowdrop flower that bloomed through a snowdrift in the bitter cold: strong, beautiful, captivating.

She walked up the steps and looked at the crown still on his head. Her eyes were very blue.

Suddenly he realized he stood in front of her in a torn, stained sweatshirt, old sweatpants, and Eeyore slippers.

"You invoked."

"I had to."

"There will be hell to pay."

She knew. No surprise there. The Wise Vasylisas knew a lot of things. All of the gods talked to them, for the Vasylisas were their instrument for preserving balance. Perhaps Morena had told her.

"It's not the first time," he told her.

"But this time it's because of my family."

Roman reached up and touched the crown. It melted into smoke, and a gust of wind carried it off. Letting go of the power was like taking off armor after a hard battle. He felt tired and calm.

She turned to Finn. "I told you before, running from these things only makes it worse."

He raised his chin.

"When the offer is made, either accept or reject it," she continued. "This neither-here-nor-there waiting to make up your mind comes with a price."

"That's fine," Finn said.

"No, it's not. You're not the one who'll be paying it. He will." She nodded at Roman.

Finn spun to Roman. "What is she talking about? What price?"

"You will see." The Vasylisa turned to Roman. "We will come with you."

"The Glades don't discriminate," he said. "They won't spare you. There is no need."

"You will be going through it because of my brother. I will go with you. It's the least I can do. He will come too. It will be good for him. He needs to know the consequences of his actions."

His mother's voice popped into Roman's head. *Karma.*

"Do you know me?" he asked.

She raised her eyebrows. A dangerous light sparked in her eyes. "You don't remember me, do you?"

He shook his head.

"Andora," she said. "Dora the Dud Explorer. Dora the Minus. I was three years behind you in the Veshnevski Academy. We had a class on runes together."

Oh gods.

"You guys went to school together?" Finn asked.

She narrowed her eyes. "I didn't have any powers back then, because the previous Vasylisa was still alive. I wasn't Slavic, I didn't speak any of the languages, and our family wasn't part of the community. I just started having strange dreams and then some manifestations happened, and the Witch Oracle found me and convinced my parents that I should be educated in Paganism."

He remembered her now. In fact, the memory was crystal clear, branded in his brain.

"Other kids were mean," Andora said. "But Roman was the meanest."

He opened his mouth. Nothing came out.

"He turned my pencils into snakes. And my shoelaces."

Somehow, he found his voice. "I was an unhappy kid. My magic was unstable. It was all snakes all the time. I couldn't control it."

"I had very long hair," she said. "It was the only thing about myself that I liked at nine years old."

Roman wished he could fade into the porch boards.

"He turned my braid into a poisonous viper."

Finn stared at him.

"It bit me. I almost died. And nobody could turn the snake back into my hair. They had to cut it off."

"I'm sorry," Roman squeezed out. It was a long time coming.

"Not yet. But you will be."

She smiled at him. Ice shot through him from his neck all the way to his feet.

"But not today. Today you saved my brother. I will collect *that* debt another time. We need to go to Nav now. You have a tree to drag."

[8]

The winter cold chilled Roman's face. He opened his eyes and shrugged, getting the harness situated across his chest.

"My friend!" Farhang floated into his field of vision. "I waited as promised."

The snow crunched, and Andora and Finn materialized on the path. Finn's shepherd puppy jumped around in the snow and frolicked, hopping up and down.

"And you've brought companions." Farhang smiled softly. "After such long solitude, this is an embarrassment of riches."

Andora glanced at Farhang. "Who is he?"

"A magav who offended his ahura."

"He tried to kill us," Finn supplied.

Farhang raised his hands. "My body did. I assure you, I'm not a threat."

Andora looked at Roman.

"He isn't," Roman agreed. "Andora, you know what is coming, so Finn and Farhang, this is mostly for you. Kid, this is the Winter Cathedral, your goddess' domain. Here she rules supreme. In the center of the Cathedral is the Ice Terem, the palace where Morena and Chernobog spend Koliada. With me so far?"

Finn nodded.

"Morena doesn't care for human visitors. To get to the palace, we must pass through her trials, the last of which are the Glades of Remembrance."

"They make you relive your worst memories," Andora said.

"If you end up serving Morena, this will be your home turf," Roman said. "You will get to skip all this and go straight to the terem. Unless you piss her off."

"Have you done it?" Finn asked.

"Oh, yes."

"More than once?"

Roman nodded. There was a reason why he was off for Koliada. Of the five times he'd had to visit the terem during the holidays at Chernobog's summons, Morena had relented only once. The other four times he'd had to go through the Glades.

"Is it the same every time?"

"Yes. Unless something even more fucked up happens, and then that will take precedence. Farhang, last chance to back out."

The magav squared his shoulders. "It's a reckoning I deserve."

Well said. Roman nodded. "Let's get this over with."

He started forward, dragging the tree across the snow.

"But what's the point of the tree?" Finn asked behind him.

"Morena and Chernobog had a spat," Roman explained. "He tried to fix it on his own, but it didn't work, so now I'm bringing her a present."

"But couldn't he just make the tree appear or get it himself?"

"No," Andora said. "The tree is not the point."

"It's the act of the dragging," Farhang said.

"I don't understand," Finn muttered.

"You need the context." Roman shifted the harness, situating it better on his shoulders. "Chernobog and Morena have a solid marriage, but occasionally, like right now, they quarrel."

"Why?" Finn asked.

"For various reasons. This time they fought because Morena wanted to kill one of Svarog's volhvs."

"Svarog is the Sky Father, the Fair Judge, the Craftsman," Andora explained. "He is the one parents pray to when they are having issues with their children, which is ironic as hell when you consider his record on parenting. He is Morena's father. Long ago, Skiper-Zmei, the Void Dragon, kidnapped Morena and her two sisters, transformed them into monsters, and forced them to commit atrocities."

Finn blinked.

"Eventually their brother Perun, the Thunderer, put together a divine squad and rescued his sisters," Roman continued. "But the gods took their sweet time getting around to it. The sisters suffered. Morena never forgave her family for abandoning her. That wail you borrowed is the sound of the anguish she felt. Her sisters, Spring and Summer, returned home, but she held a grudge, so she went into Nav, met Chernobog, they fell in love, and she married him. Your goddess has a temper. There are times when she loses it, and her husband has to…"

He eyed the woods in case they decided to turn angry, but the snow lay placid.

"Talk her off a cliff," Andora finished for him. "A week ago, one of Svarog's volhvs made a speech during the early Koliada rites, went off on a tangent about children and parents, and called Morena ungrateful."

"She isn't ungrateful. She was abandoned," Finn growled.

"True," Roman agreed. "Svarog's volhv has issues with his son. I don't know what Alexander did this time to piss his father off, but his old man apparently decided to get some things off his chest and used Morena to do it. It was unwise. Your goddess wanted to remind them exactly where they stood. Chernobog kept her from doing something rash. Now he is hoping to calm the winter storm with a gift. But it can't be any old gift. It has to be something special."

"So, the tree is special?"

"No, but I am," Roman said.

"And so humble." Andora looked to the sky.

"For the first five years I served Chernobog, Morena found some reason for me to be summoned to the Ice Terem during Koliada. I've gone through the Glades four times. In my sixth year I did my god a great service."

"What was it?" Finn asked.

"I killed a Void monster in his name. His power got a big boost, and he granted me a boon," Roman said. "I'm not to be called upon during Koliada. Especially not on this day. He broke his promise to me to show his wife that he treasures her so much he would rather fight with me than with her. This tree is proof of his devotion and my obeisance."

"What if you don't do it?" Finn asked. "What if you just stop?"

"I can't. The tree is the price of invoking Chernobog's name. He lent me his crown, his bow, and his power. In return, I will drag this fir all the way to the Ice Terem, and I will not complain. I have many faults, Finn, but I am a man of my word."

Roman grinned and pulled harder.

THE WOODS HAD LOST THEIR GRIMNESS. A GODFIRE SUNRISE PLAYED across the sky, glowing with pink, then lavender, then a gentle purple with gossamer trails of turquoise brilliance stretching across like shimmering veils. It was neither night nor day, but a magical time in between, and the farther they went, the brighter the sky grew. Morena was in a better mood. He was bringing her a pretty tree, and her new priest was coming home.

They kept walking. Farhang and Finn had fallen slightly behind, Farhang trying to explain Zoroastrianism and a magav's powers. Andora caught up with him and kept pace through the snow.

"Cold?" he asked.

She shook her head.

"About those two with the wheel and the weird magic," he said. "Do you know where they came from?"

Andora shook her head again. "Never came across anything like that."

Another mystery to add to his to-do list.

They strode side by side. Now was as good a time as any.

"Look, about the whole snake thing..."

She raised her eyebrows at him. The woman could cut with a look like nobody he'd ever met.

"It's my fault," he said. "I did it. I just want to clarify that it wasn't intentional bullying."

"Then what was it?"

"Proximity and lack of control."

She rolled her eyes. "Oh, I can't wait to hear this."

He gathered himself.

"Well?"

"Hang on. I stuffed all my feelings down like a proper man, and it takes some effort to bring them back up."

"Take your time."

Roman sighed. "I was a really unhappy twelve-year-old."

"You said that part."

"My parents were separating. They'd separated a couple of times before, but this time it felt different. Final."

His parents had never married, although his mother introduced herself as Mrs. Tihomirov to this day when the occasion called for it. Now, after years of watching them clash and make up, he was sure they would never leave each other. Age had mellowed them both enough to live in the same house most of the time, and their fights had lost much of their former viciousness. But back then, it was chaos.

"My sisters were panicking. It felt like the family was collapsing. Mom and Dad had tried to shield us from their problems as much as they could, but they were angry with each other. My brother was…"

"A shithead."

"Perfect. He was perfect. He was seven years older, and he was good at everything. He was at the top of every class. Theoretical, practical, didn't matter. Top three with a spear, number one with a bow. He was a sniper. When he went hunting, even if everyone else came back empty-handed, he would always bring home game. I never had patience for the bow."

"You seemed to do fine half an hour ago," she said.

"Years of practice. To my brother, it came naturally. I once asked him how he did it, and he told me to stop thinking. Make myself empty. Don't be bored, don't be worried. Just be empty, and wait."

She sighed.

"My brother never got in trouble. No matter what the task was, he would do it properly every time, exceeding expectations, while I couldn't put a foot right. I came from a prominent magical family. I had to uphold our reputation. Great things were expected of me, and somehow everything I touched turned to shit."

"Ah yes, the poor little pagan prince," Andora said, but her words didn't have any bite to them.

"In my first semester of the fifth grade, I ended up in the principal's office more times than my brother had ever been in his entire twelve years at the Academy. It had gotten to the point where, when I got in trouble, they would call him for the parent-teacher talk. He never got angry. He never berated. He just looked at me like I was a maggot. Like he had expected me to amount to nothing, so there was no point in being disappointed."

"That's a lot of feelings," Andora said. "Are you going to be alright?"

"No worries, after this is done, I will put them back where they belong, and we won't talk about this again. Ever."

"Well, at least you have a plan." Her tone told him his plan was stupid.

He really didn't want to keep going, but he was doing this, in part, to atone. If a member of the faith had come to him for spiritual guidance in this matter, he would have advised them to talk to the injured party and to unburden themself. There was a cost to that, because to do it properly meant to lay himself bare. Forgiveness would come or it would not, but, as Farhang had said, this was the reckoning he deserved.

Although right now it didn't feel like unburdening would help much.

"Anyway, it was decided early on that my brother would become the Black Volhv after my father. My parents always said it was his right as the firstborn."

"But there is no such rule, is there?" she asked softly.

"No." He scrounged for the right words. "Men make plans, but gods pull the strings of fate. I was a soft-hearted kid. When I was about five, our cat got hit by a car, and I found him on the side of the road, dead."

He could still vividly remember the ice-cold rush when he saw the mangled body.

"I cried for a really long time, to the point where they took me to a therapist to see if there was something wrong."

"What did the therapist say?"

"She said I was sad. Gods become attached to a particular bloodline. It's familiar, and they are creatures of habit. It was clear that Chernobog would choose his priest from our family, and neither of my parents thought I could handle it. They thought I was too soft, and that serving Chernobog would kill me. That I would end up like some of the others who tried to be Black Volhvs and, as my dad once put it years later, be found hanging from some branch with a vacuum cord around my neck. If anyone could carry that burden, it would be my brother, who had his shit together. He was...colder. Less affected by things. Better suited to our particular brand of priesthood. And he wanted it. It felt like the best decision for everyone, and they were determined to stick to it."

"Parents mean well," Andora said.

"They do." Roman shrugged, the tree a steady weight behind him. "My earliest memory is from Nav."

She glanced at him.

"I don't know how old I was. Young. Maybe three. I was outside. It was dark, but there was this big fire burning. A giant man sat by the fire. He was cooking meat on skewers, and he gave me one. It was so delicious. It was too hot to touch, but I couldn't eat it fast enough. The man watched me and chuckled."

Andora's eyes went wide. "You made—"

"Shhh," he told her.

"You made *him* laugh?" she murmured.

He'd gotten more than one chuckle out of Chernobog, but it wasn't something to talk about.

"After that, I didn't visit for a long time. I had convinced myself that I'd imagined it, and then I turned ten and the dreams started. By that point I knew enough to put two and two together. Like it or not, I was wandering through Nav at night. Eventually I told my dad, and he lost it. Looking back on it, I think it scared him, and he was trying to protect me, but what I got out of it was that I, an epic screw-up, was trying to steal my perfect brother's glorious destiny."

"Ugh." She shook her head. "The guilt."

"Yeah. I couldn't stop dreaming no matter how hard I tried. By twelve, I had run around Nav so much, it was like coming home. I was getting weird powers, and my magic was erratic. My parents' separation put a cherry on top of that cake. I started failing my classes. It felt like I kept falling into a hole and couldn't get out of it."

They were almost out of the forest. Another half mile and the Glades would begin. He had to get to the point.

"I would sit around and brood. The more I brooded, the darker things seemed, the more my magic bucked against it. The first time the snakes happened, I had failed a quiz. My brother had warned me just that morning not to do anything that would aggravate Mom or Dad. So I sat there, trying to think of some way to hide the bad grade and the more I thought, the angrier I got, and the harder it was to keep a hold of my magic, until it exploded."

"Aha. It just happened. Of course. It couldn't possibly be your fault."

"It was my fault, but it wasn't targeted at you. It was omnidirectional. I sat in the last row, in the corner. There was nobody to my left or behind me. Dabrowski sat in front of me. Daciana sat to my right. You sat in front of Daciana. Dabrowski has a natural resistance to Nav- and Prav-based magic. Something to do with his nature-based powers. They peg him as neutral and fail to notice he is there."

"Mhm."

"Daciana always carried so many protective charms, her belt was like one of those baby mobiles. You didn't have anything. It makes sense now, looking at it as an adult, but at the time I had no clue. When your pencils turned into snakes, I didn't even know what I did. I couldn't undo it, I tried. I told them I didn't mean to, but nobody believed me, since I had a school rap sheet a mile long."

She gave him a skeptical glance.

"My parents were called. It was a big deal. The second time, I realized what happened as it was happening, so I looked down to try to contain it. I ended up looking at your shoes. And then you had shoelace snakes, and I went back to the office. My mother talked to me, my father talked to me, everyone talked to me. Everyone explained how I couldn't keep doing this crap. My father put a bone charm on a cord and told me to always wear it around my neck."

"Mhm. And the third time?"

"The third time was...intentional. Again, not targeted at you specifically, but intentional." He could still recall the splash of boiling hot anger that overtook him.

"What happened? Something must've happened."

"It wasn't good."

"You've come this far, Roman. Let's have all of it."

There was no escape. He sighed.

"The night before, Lena, one of my sisters, was doing her homework. She was always a good artist, and she was drawing portraits of Nav's gods. She gave Chernobog a longbow. I told her that wasn't what the bow looked like. I had seen it up close. I'd held it and fired it, although I kept that part to myself. She didn't believe me. I had a teenage moment. You know when you're twelve, and you are absolutely certain that you're right and the world is trying to wrong you? I dragged her to my brother, all indignant, because I knew my father had taken him to see Chernobog, too, and, as the future Black Volhv, he would settle this."

"And?"

"I didn't know it at the time, but when my father and brother had gone before Chernobog, he'd looked at my brother, said two words, and sent them back out."

"And what were they?" she prompted.

"'Wrong boy.'"

Andora let out a short laugh.

"My brother knew me really well. He'd watched me get in trouble with the school enough times, and he could tell I wasn't lying. He realized that I must've seen the bow. A light bulb went off in his head."

"He'd figured out the right boy."

"He did. He looked at me, and there was hatred in his eyes. I saw it. It was like a physical thing. He'd said, 'Aren't you tired of being a fuck-up? Every day you shame our family. Nobody wants to hear anything that comes out of your mouth. Learn to be silent. That's the best thing for you.'"

He remembered it word for word.

"Wow."

They had reached the end of the woods. The Glades waited ahead, a wide opening, wrapped in a wall of forest. Roman stopped. Andora stopped, too.

"I didn't sleep that night. I just got angrier and angrier. In the morning, I went to school, and I don't remember most of the day. I sat at my desk and stewed in my rage. I was so pissed off, it felt like I went blind. I hadn't asked for any of this. I was tired of trying my best. They thought I was a fuck-up, so I would be a fuck-up." He took a deep breath. "I let go. Because that's what fuck-ups do. I didn't care if anybody got hurt. I just pushed it all out. All the hate, all the anger. All the bad feelings. My dad's bone charm turned red, burned through my clothes, and broke. And then you had a viper instead of hair. I felt terrible. I still feel terrible."

"You never apologized."

"I'm sorry."

"No, Roman. Back then, when we were kids. You never apologized."

"I punched Kovalyev when he was laughing about it."

She stared at him. "Punching an unrelated third party doesn't count as an apology."

"They moved you out of our class. I was told to not come within fifty feet of you."

"You could've found a way." Her voice was merciless.

"I could've," he admitted. "I didn't know what to say. That's why I left chocolate in your desk."

She blinked. "That was you? I thought it was Lisa."

"Lisa would've left you gummy bears."

"True."

"Again, the blame is mine. I just want to be clear that it wasn't personal in any way. Ask Dabrowski when we get back to my house. That last one made him sick as a dog. He vomited for like an hour, and Daciana passed out. So I wasn't picking on you. I wasn't trying to get your attention. I didn't derive any happiness from tormenting you. I had so much of my own shit going on, I barely registered the fact that you existed."

"Ouch." She laughed a little.

"I'm digging this hole deeper, aren't I?"

"Oh yes. What kind of chocolate was it?"

"Ferrero Rocher," he said. "With hazelnuts. Golden wrappers. Sixteen in a pack."

Chocolate was expensive in the Post-Shift world. He had spent everything he'd had on it.

She sighed.

"Were they good?"

Andora nodded. "They were. But it doesn't make up for the hair."

"Tell me what I can do," he said.

She glanced at him.

"I'm serious. Whatever I can do to say I'm sorry, I'll do it."

"Mmm, it's so lovely."

"What?"

"The sound of your groveling." She grinned at him. "I'm quite enjoying this."

He didn't know what to say to that.

"I have something in mind. Let's get through this first." She closed her mouth, then changed her mind. "Did they punish you? Your parents?"

"They didn't have to," he said. "I was miserable enough already. My sister had spilled the beans about the bow, too. Within a week, they got a place for my brother, and he moved out on his own. The school never called my brother again. I didn't get in as much trouble from that point on, but when something did happen, my dad would come in his black robes to glare at the principal."

He chuckled softly at the memory.

"My dad talked to me for a while and told me I wasn't worthless and that what happened was his fault for not paying attention. My uncle, the White Volhv, made a warding circle out of gold and hung it on the wall by my bed. It cost our family an arm and a leg, but the Nav dreams stopped after that."

"And that's how your father betrayed his god," she murmured.

He nodded.

An ancient conflict existed between Chernobog and Belobog. They were brothers and rivals. His father had done the unforgivable. He wasn't the one who'd gone to the White Volhv for help—it was his mother. But he had allowed the warding circle that was made with Belobog's magic to be hung in Roman's bedroom to sever the connection between Chernobog and his future chosen.

"Why do you think he did it?" she asked.

"My father seems arrogant and abrasive."

"Yes, I've met the man." She made a face.

"'Seems' is the key word here. There is a reason my mother can't quit him. He is a lot like my brother but a lot like me, too. We both got something from him. So, when it came to the circle, some of it was out of love. He honestly believed that doing Chernobog's bidding would kill me. And some of it was stubbornness."

Andora sighed. "You don't say."

"There are many Black Volhvs. We're not unique like Vasylisas. When a pagan community gets large enough, it gets one. But of all of the Black Volhvs serving Chernobog across the world, my father was his favorite. He wielded a lot of power, and he'd done things in his god's name that haunt him still. In his mind, he'd asked for very little. Chernobog wanted one of my father's sons to serve him. Fine. He obliged, chose a son he thought was best suited, and offered him to his god. The least his god could do was to respect my father's choice. And when Chernobog didn't, my father dug his heels in."

His father had served faithfully for many decades, so Chernobog hadn't killed him. He had simply stopped speaking to him. If a Black Volhv managed to survive to a ripe old age, they gracefully retired, letting their successors do more and more of the work, but they never lost their connection to their god. They were honored and feared, up to the moment of their death. Instead, his brother had been forced to take over everything at once, and then it all went sideways.

Nobody outside the family knew what really happened. Except, apparently, for Andora, who had a direct line to Morena and probably to Chernobog as well. Even Roman himself hadn't known for years that his father had been cut off. He'd learned about it during that desperate late-night phone call that had ended his military career and brought him back to Atlanta for good. This was a secret he was determined to keep. Grigorii Semionovich Tihomirov would live the rest of his life as the Black Volhv, if in name only.

"There is not much left to the story," Roman said. "I kept my head down, made it through school with half decent grades, and then enlisted as soon as I could. The next... Well, you know what happened next."

Ahead, the snow sheathing the Glades glittered like diamonds. Thin wisps of magic swirled just above the ground, picking up stray snowflakes and spinning them into miniature tornados. No escape.

"This is going to be hell," she said.

"Nah." He grinned. "Hell is for Christians and the Norse. For us, it's just another day in Nav."

Roman squared his shoulders and pulled the tree into the open.

———

THE WISPS OF MAGIC SPARKLED WITH BRILLIANT LIGHT, LIKE GLITTER caught in a sunbeam. Roman watched them, mentally bracing himself. They'd been walking through the Glades for about thirty seconds. You never knew when the magic would hit. Sometimes it barely let him take a couple of steps, and sometimes he was almost to the line of trees at the other end and thinking he was in the clear when it dragged him back in.

On the left, a couple of tiny tornadoes merged and fell apart. A shape began to coalesce on the snow.

Farhang paled.

The shape came into focus. A young woman of unforgettable beauty, with big brown eyes and a waterfall of long slender dark braids. She wore a flowing dress, and her face was heartbreakingly sad.

Farhang's feet hit the ground, and he walked toward her through the snow like a man possessed.

Here we go.

She looked at him, and there were tears in her eyes. "Help us, Farhang."

"I'm here," he said.

Her braids looked like something Uzbek women wore. The patterns on her dress might have come from that region too, a modern take on an ikat. The original conversation probably wasn't in English, but it didn't matter. The language of Morena's illusion was universal.

Two more shapes materialized, born from snowflakes and magic, two young girls, one a teenager and the other maybe ten. Their faces echoed that of the first woman. She was too young to be their mother, so she must've been their sister.

"You will keep us safe, won't you?"

"I will," Farhang promised.

His mouth shaped the words, but his eyes filled with pain. The real Farhang, the one inside, knew it was a memory and was breaking down as the magic compelled him to repeat the words he'd said in the past.

That was the bitter, twisted nature of the Glades' magic. It pulled your memories out and compelled you to reenact them, over and over, like some sort of nightmarish play.

"We don't have anyone. Nobody can help us, except you. Your powers are so strong, Farhang."

"Please protect us," the teenage girl said.

"I swear on my life that I will kill the spawn of Ahriman before he claims you," Farhang said. "Let Mithra witness my vow. Should I break this covenant, let my very being be torn asunder."

And so it was. Mithra was the deity of covenants, contracts, and justice. A vow in his name would be enforced.

"But you failed, didn't you, Farhang?" the youngest child said. "You failed."

"You promised," the teenager said.

"You bragged," the young woman said. "You swore and postured."

"I'm so sorry, Mohira," Farhang said, his voice brimming with pain. "I'm so sorry."

"Not enough. Look what your hubris wrought. Look at what's become of us."

Mohira's mouth opened and kept opening, splitting her head nearly in half. Her human teeth fell out. Long triangular fangs sprouted from her gums.

Grief contorted Farhang's face.

Her clothes tore. For a moment she was nude and human, and then her limbs stretched, growing longer, thinner. Her hands became clawed paws. Her stomach collapsed inward, her human hips shifted, her neck elongated, carrying the head up. Scales sheathed her flanks, splattered with blobs of eye-pain-inducing orange and ultramarine and striped with deep black, the kind of colors usually found on poisonous frogs and venomous snakes. A second pair of eyes opened on the sides of her head, next to the first ones.

The nightmarish creature landed on the snow on all fours. Its build, lean and designed for speed, reminded Roman of a cheetah, but there was something reptilian about her, besides the scales—something that set off an instinctual alarm at the base of his neck.

The two younger girls metamorphosed in unison.

The Mohira-monster licked her fangs with a long lizard tongue, dripping with foul spit. A shrill voice issued from her maw, like nails on a chalkboard.

"I hate you!"

Farhang took a step back.

"I will kill you! I will rip you apart! I want you to hurt and suffer! I will make you suffer!"

Finn raised his hands.

Roman grabbed him by the shoulder. "No."

"But..."

"No. This is not your fight."

"He's right," Andora said. "Don't interfere."

The monsters launched themselves at Farhang. Magic flared around his hands, a radiant corona of fire. He screamed as if cut, and a jet of flames tore from him. The creatures darted around him, too fast, as his fire struck again and again, missing them by inches.

Farhang's fire looked hot enough to melt the world, but the blanket of snow sheathing the Glades remained pristine and unbothered.

The teenager was the first to fall. She'd gotten too cocky, and the fire caught her right flank. The flames burned a hole in her side, exposing pale ribs. The stench of cooked flesh spread through the clearing. Finn gagged.

The injured monster fell onto the snow, screaming. The other two screeched in unison.

It took a long time. Ten minutes, maybe twelve. An eternity in a fight. Farhang fought as hard as he could, his magic a firestorm, then a purifying shower, as he tried and failed to purge the corrupting magic from their dying bodies. And then he wept.

They waited for the shudders to die down. Finally, he got up and walked over to them on unsteady legs, looking like a risen corpse. He took his place next to Finn, and they resumed their trek.

They managed to take less than a dozen steps when Andora strode away from them into the snow, toward a magic whirlwind. A group of people appeared in the open. On one side, a woman in her late twenties held a boy, maybe two or three years old. She clutched the boy to her as if afraid someone would rip him out of her arms. Across from her, a group of six people waited, their faces grim.

Among the six, an older woman wore a gray robe with Troyan's symbol on it, one triangle on the bottom, three on top. Troyan was the Healer, a Nav god who ruled over disease. His devotees healed the sick. Next to the healer, a young woman wore an amulet with Makosh's twisted spiral—a seer, possibly an oracle.

"You must kill the child," Troyan's priestess intoned.

The mother of the boy hugged him tighter to herself. He had big blue eyes, chubby cheeks, and a head of reddish-blond hair. He almost looked like a bewildered kitten that was snatched off the floor in the middle of playing and now had no idea what was going on.

"He is barely three years old," Andora said.

"He will be the death of all of us. The entire town will die," Troyan's priestess said.

"The child is innocent. At this point, he hasn't done anything," Andora repeated. "You're asking me to take a life because of something you think might happen."

"Will happen!" Troyan's priestess pointed toward Makosh's seer.

"It will come to pass," the seer said.

"Last year your uncle, Sergei Ivanovich, predicted that the winter would be so cold, birds would freeze in flight," Andora said. "Instead, you had record warm temperatures. Three years ago, you predicted that Red Rock Bridge would collapse. It is still standing."

"This is different," the seer said.

"Please!" The mother's voice shook. "He's just a little boy!"

"Their whole family are Lihoradka's worshippers," a man called out. "We should burn them all."

Andora unsheathed her sword. "There will be no witch hunts."

The man stepped back.

She turned to the mother clutching at her son. "I won't let anyone hurt him, or you. Go home."

The woman fled and vanished.

Andora faced the gathering. "I don't care what you foresaw. This is America. We do not punish people because they might do something. You are presumed innocent until you're proven guilty. I'm telling you right now, if anyone touches a hair on that child's head, I will come back and make you regret it. Do not test me."

Magic and snow swirled. A field of corpses filled the Glade. They slumped on the ground in contorted poses, their lips gone, their teeth exposed. Holes peppered their faces as if something had taken bites out of their flesh. Sores filled with pus split the remaining skin.

In the center of it all, a child sat on a heap of bodies. He had grown. He was maybe five or six now. His hair had turned lighter and more blond, and he had lost the chubby cheeks, but the eyes were the same, round and blue. He saw Andora and cackled.

"Do you like it?"

She didn't say anything.

"I couldn't have done it if it wasn't for you. Oooh, poor baby me. So cute and adorable. And you, so fierce. 'Nobody will touch the child, or I will come back and punish you.' You stupid, stupid bitch."

He grinned and kicked the nearest corpse, whose symbol of Troyan was still visible despite the pus and bodily fluids.

"Thirty-seven. That's how many I killed. Thirty-seven. And

you will be the thirty-eighth. But I'll kill your soul first. Thank you so much for all your help."

The boy raised his hand. A larger phantom hand overlaid his, its fingers long and bony, its claws dripping grayish slime. Lihoradka's hand.

Behind him, bodies shifted. Corpses rose, their eyes glowing with greenish fire, like foul swamp lights.

Andora plunged her sword into the ground. He didn't hear the incantation, but he knew whom she reached out to for help. Before you eradicated disease you had to contain it, and who better than a goddess who already held a grudge against the culprit?

Finn gaped at the iceberg sheathing the clearing. The ice was clear as glass, and within it, the boy hung unmoving, caught in mid-leap as he'd tried to escape. His frozen blue eyes brimmed with fear.

"This is how to do it properly," Roman told Finn. "See, she freezes and holds. You need to work on the holding part."

The iceberg melted, and fire spun through the glade, turning bodies into candles.

Andora returned. Her eyes were red. She didn't say anything. She just stared straight ahead.

The tiny magic whirlwinds danced across the snow.

Roman unbuckled his harness and stepped away from the tree.

"Don't," Andora said. "Maybe she will let you pass."

"She won't. Might as well get it over with."

He walked into the snow and waited.

The snowflakes swirled. He was seeing it for the fifth time, and he caught the precise moment they snapped into the familiar shape. He walked across the snow, tall, slender, his face grim, his dark hair expertly cut. He was exactly as Roman remembered, down to his black robes with its embroidered hem. Roman had a set just like it, except his embroidery was silver, not glowing with deep, raging purple.

"Why can't I get away from you?" Rodion asked. "You came into this world screaming, a loud, obnoxious thing, smelling of piss and shit. Everyone was showing you off, and I looked at you and thought, 'It would only take a pinch to smother you.' I could just reach out and squeeze. I should've drowned you when you were a baby."

This was the part when he would ask, "Why didn't you?" and Rodion would say, "I would get caught, stupid." Except, for some odd reason, Roman didn't feel compelled to follow the script.

"What going on?" Finn asked behind him.

"Roman's brother was a psychopath," Andora said. "He only cared about power, and when he became the Black Volhv, the dark magic seduced him. There are things in Nav and on the border with the Void that feed on human desires. If you let them, they will claim you."

"You are the reason Mom and Dad separated," Rodion said. "I never chose sides. I let them handle their own problems, but you, no, you had to wedge your way between them with your opinions on what was fair and not fair."

The words just didn't have that vicious bite they'd always had. The tone was the same, the hatred on Rodion's face was the same, but somehow it didn't hurt like it used to.

The evil thing that was Rodion waited for him to respond.

"What happened?" Finn asked.

"Rodion started passing judgements. He killed some people, and he would summon dark things to do his bidding," Andora said. "The Black Volhv is supposed to intercede on people's behalf. Instead, he terrorized them."

"What about Chernobog?"

"He let it happen," she said.

It was punishment. For their father and for the entire congregation. Chernobog had made his wishes known, and they were ignored. So, he let things take their natural course. He didn't feed Rodion's rampage, but he did not restrain it.

"You're the reason Alyona died—"

"Their father tried to stop Rodion and got hurt. Rodion withdrew to Nav."

Defiance required penance.

"—you're like a fucking cockroach that's too stupid to die—"

"The family called Roman. On this day, twelve years ago, Roman went into Nav and killed his brother."

The torrent of verbal venom Rodion had leveled at him was still washing over him, but the guilt was no longer there. He still remembered this confrontation in excruciating detail, the fight, the vicious dark magic tainted with the Void that had boiled out of his brother and torn at him with phantom teeth, the black blade that had appeared in his own hand, the hiss it made as it slid into Rodion's chest, and Chernobog's voice, which sounded like the end of the world as he said an ancient greeting that was recognition, announcement, and acknowledgement rolled into one.

"**GOI ESI, ROMAN, MOY VOLHV.**"

Alive you are, Roman, my volhv.

There was no guilt anymore. No pain. Just acceptance. It took five tries, but he finally got the point.

Ha.

"—you were always a shit smear on the family's name and now you think that by coming here you can do—"

"Look, dickhead," Roman interrupted. "I'd like to stay and chat, but I have a tree to drag."

He turned around and walked away.

A wail of rage screeched behind him. He felt the furious darkness streak to him, ready to rip him to pieces. But he was the Black Volhv. Roman waved his hand, not bothering to face the threat. It vanished, snuffed out of existence. The Glades became bright and empty.

He walked over to the fir, slipped the harness back on, and started toward the distant woods. The tree felt so light, it was as if it were floating behind him.

EPILOGUE

The woods parted. A snowy plain unrolled in front of them. A frozen river flowed through it, coiling in a ring, its surface slick like glass and a deep midnight-blue. In the loop of the river, poised against the distant forest and low, snow-capped mountains, a terem rose.

Crafted from pure white snow with huge, oval windows and panels of light blue ice, it perched upon the island like a fantastic, many-tiered wedding cake of a building. Six towers of various heights and widths thrust toward the sky, each more ornate than the last, their cupolas frosted with crushed teal ice and topped with ice spires that looked like sword blades. Lavish balconies with carved rails hugged the towers, snaking between them at different heights. A bridge stretched in a graceful curve across the water to the shore.

Finally. Roman sped up.

The moment his foot touched the bridge, the harness binding him to the tree fell apart in a flurry of snowflakes.

A star detached from the top balcony and sped over their heads to land in the snow. A miniature winter storm swirled where it landed, and from it Morena stepped out. She stood ten feet tall, a woman with the face of a goddess, her skin white as snow, two long braids, black as the winter sky, snaking down her chest. A kokoshnik tiara crowned her brow, glittering with blue and white diamonds. She wore a sarafan, a long dress with a voluminous pale blue skirt, and a shuba, a long winter coat with a white fur collar, cinched to her waist with a silver belt.

Her eyes shone with the blue of the brightest godfire. Looking into them was like being punched off your feet—Winter looked back, merciless, breathtaking, and frightening.

She had gone with the classic image today. First impressions were important. Judging by the look on Finn's face, it worked. The kid was shocked into silence.

Yes, yes, just wait until you see her earlier iteration, the one with unbrushed hair, wrapped in furs, and devouring raw meat with a mouth full of ice fangs. She didn't revert to that form too often now, but once in a while, it made an appearance.

Morena raised an arm. The shepherd puppy leapt forward, changing shape in mid-jump. A black swan with glowing ruby eyes landed on Morena's forearm and rubbed her head against Morena's shoulder.

The fir tree rose on its own, floated across the lake, and landed on the large crescent balcony, touching down with a peal of thunder. Ornaments sprouted on the branches: small sculptures of animals fashioned from ice with startling accuracy; glittering jewels and treasures from Morena's vaults; intricate silver chains that only Chernobog could weave; icicles that sparkled like diamonds; bright red berries; golden pinecones; and atop it all, Morena's sigil encrusted with gems. Little motes of godfire, green, blue, and pink ignited in the branches.

Wow. She'd pulled out all the stops.

The goddess nodded at Andora and turned to the boy.

"WELCOME, FINN," Morena said.

The kid gaped.

A wolf the size of a horse trotted out of the woods, all pale fur and teeth. He lay on the ground in front of Finn.

"THIS IS BURAN. HE WILL GIVE YOU A TOUR OF MY HOME. WAIT FOR ME THERE."

Finn blinked at Buran.

"She means for you to ride the wolf," Roman told him.

"I've ridden him before," Andora said. "He's nice."

Roman almost choked on empty air. The first time he'd seen Buran, he was up North in the human world, near the Great Lakes. It had been a quiet winter day, soft and fuzzy. Light powdery snowflakes sifted down. Suddenly, fat chunks of snow rained from the sky. Wind howled, the snow-covered field mixed with the snow-smudged sky, and the world vanished into a blinding blizzard. And then, as he'd held his arm up to try to shield his face, a giant form emerged from the raging storm, locked his teeth on Roman's arm, and yanked him straight into Nav, because Morena had wanted a word.

Buran turned his shaggy head and looked at Finn.

Finn's eyes widened. He climbed onto the beast, and the wolf took off like a bullet across the bridge. The swan leaped off Morena's arm, turning back into a shepherd in a blink, and chased Finn and the wolf.

Morena leveled her gaze at Roman. **"Such a simple lesson, and it took you so long."**

"Five times," he said. "I'm slow, but I can be taught."

The goddess smiled. **"Foolish boy. If there is one thing I cannot stand, it is to see a man enslaved. Especially by his own guilt."**

He knew.

"You are my gift to my husband on this Koliada. Now you can be all he wishes you to be."

"I'm honored," Roman said.

"Well, he deserves it. He loves me so."

Morena reached into her wide sleeve and withdrew a delicate

ice fruit. The Winter Apple, glowing softly with blue and white. A kiss from a goddess, a blank check for a single wish.

"**You've done well bringing the boy to me.**"

She dropped the apple into Roman's palm.

Any boon he wanted.

Roman studied the apple.

Any boon within her ability to grant.

He glanced at Morena.

"**Are you sure? You know I don't hand many of these out.**"

"I'm sure," he said.

Morena shook her head. "**The softest heart aches the hardest, Roman.**"

"I promise to harden mine after this."

The goddess sighed and flicked her fingers. The apple streaked to Farhang and broke over him in a shower of snowflakes. The space behind the magav split, yawned, slurped him out of Nav, and snapped shut.

A vast dark shadow loomed in the wide doorway that led to the tree and the balcony. His black cloak swirled about him. The glow of Morena's tree lights played on his scale armor. The God of the Final End stepped onto the balcony.

Time to test the waters. Roman met his god's gaze.

Angry?

The left corner of Chernobog's severe mouth quirked. The answer exploded in Roman's mind.

YOU ARE MY VOLHV.

A strange feeling filled Roman. It was as if the world had been tilted slightly off-kilter, and now it suddenly righted itself. Power coursed through him, bringing relief, peace, and hope.

Morena gave him a sharp smile.

"**You two should go. I will send Finn to you after we speak.**"

Nav tore in half.

Roman opened his eyes. He stood on his porch.

Potholes covered the yard, the ground plowed here and there

by random tracks, some still oozing with ichor. The remnants of the bone hands stuck out of the dirt. The porch was a mess of shattered boards, scarred with burns from the yellow goo. The front window lay shattered in his living room. The door and the front wall were full of holes.

And they still didn't know where the priest and the warrior had come from or if whoever sent them would try again.

He sighed.

The door behind him creaked. Farhang stumbled out into the daylight, his face bright and bewildered. The pack of nechist spilled out onto the porch with him, Roro in the lead.

"I am...myself." Farhang grinned at Roman. "I am myself, my friend!"

He scooped one of the kolovershi up and spun around with it. The little beast squealed. Farhang let it go and half-ran, half-jumped onto the yard, flinging his arms wide.

The kolovershi followed. Roro thought about it, sidled up to Andora instead, and licked her hand. *"Roro."*

Andora absentmindedly petted Roro's head.

The iron hound slunk out onto the porch, hesitant. Behind him, the anchutka crawled out, blinking at the sunlight.

Farhang laughed, making weird little circles.

"How long did you say he was stuck?" Andora asked.

"Three years, he thinks."

"Ah. That would explain the frolicking."

Farhang wandered down the driveway, hopped over a puddle of goo that used to be the mercenary sniper, and took off into the woods, spinning his arms. The kolovershi trailed him, clearly concerned.

"They won't let him wander too far off," Roman told her.

The house behind them creaked. They turned to look at it.

Darkness slithered up the walls. The glass shards lifted from the floor and reassembled into a window. The holes in the door and the porch closed. The yellow goo vanished, leaving unscarred stone in its wake. The house was as it had been. The yard was still a mess, though, but he was not one to look a gift from a god in its mouth.

Thank you.

"I guess you are forgiven for your tantrum," Andora said.

"You know about that, too?"

"Oh, I watched it. It was a glorious rant." She laughed softly.

"Did Morena show it to you?"

"Wouldn't you like to know."

"Do all the gods talk to you?" he asked, resigned.

"Most of them. Some more than others. I'm starving. I don't suppose you have anything to eat?"

"There might be some leftovers." Roman said. "I had eggnog and cookies but the nechist stole them all."

"Do you have the ingredients, Roman?"

"Um…"

"Eggs, sugar, cream? Things like that?"

"Yes."

Andora nodded. "I will make you cookies and eggnog. It will give us time to chat while Finn and Morena finish talking."

He opened his mouth to say something.

"It's Koliada, after all. We must at least have cookies." Andora nodded to him. "Come on, Black Volhv. Show me your pantry. We will be going to visit your family tonight. You will need cookies *and* eggnog to get through it."

The End

130

KIND REGARDS

"Ignat Trofimovich?"

Svarog's volhv raised his head from the accounting book. The young volhv-in-training hovered near the door to his office, unsure. The look on his face said, *something bad happened.*

This entire holiday season had been one disaster after another.

First, the temple treasurer disappeared. A review of their accounts found she had embezzled fifty thousand dollars over the last three years. The loss of money was insulting, but not that painful. Their smiths were the best in the entire south. They weren't hurting for money. Unfortunately, the woman had administrative access to the entire computer system, the calendar, the accounting, and the banking, and she had locked them out before she left. It was taking his IT people ages to restore access.

Then, his sister-in-law decided she wanted a divorce. His brother determined that the best way to deal with it was getting sloppy drunk every other day and coming to Ignat's office to cry about his sorrows.

Finally, after years of causing all sorts of grief, his own son decided to put him into an early grave by nearly giving him a stroke. A week ago, Alexander had gotten up after the service and announced that he had finally found his calling in life. He would become a werewolf and join the Pack. And when he was asked why, he had the audacity to claim that their congregation had lost their way and the only path to restoring true worship was to become one with the animals.

Ignat fixed the young volhv with his heavy stare. "What is it? An earthquake? A meteor shower? A dragon?"

"A teenager," the volhv said. "And a wolf."

"Is it one of the Pack's people? Are they here for Alexander?"

"No," the volhv mumbled.

"Did this teenager say what he wanted?"

"To talk to you."

"Tell him I'm busy."

The volhv shifted from foot to foot.

"What?" Ignat asked.

"It's a very large wolf."

Ignat threw the pen on his desk and stood up. Clearly, he would have to handle this himself.

"Fetch me my hammer."

The apprentice volhv ran out.

His office lay at the very back of Svarog's kapisheh, a Slavic pagan temple, and as Ignat crossed the massive wooden hall, his shoulders relaxed. The place was a marvel of carpentry, with hand-carved columns and ornate fretwork. The huge stained glass windows depicted famous scenes from Svarog's legends: Svarog with his hammer in the Sky Forge, Svarog gifting humans the plow, Svarog forging the first Bulat Steel sword...

As much as Ignat hated to admit it, Alexander did have a point, in a roundabout way. Historically, the worship of Slavic deities took place outside. Formal temples like this kapisheh were rare. But they were living in modern times, and Svarog was the Crafter, the Sky Smith. It was only fair that they built this handsome hall for him, with the smithies attached, and it was only right that this is where they worshipped the Sky Father. They'd really achieved something here. There was beauty in it. Real craftsmanship.

Ignat patted the ornate column as he passed. He admitted to himself that he might have gotten a bit heated during that one early Koliada rite, but he would be damned if he allowed the rantings of a spoiled, ungrateful child to shake the foundations of *his* congregation. That kind of shit-stirring needed to be stopped at the start before balance was lost. Alexander would get over it. Not the first time he'd been made into a public example.

Ignat reached the front entrance. The apprentice volhv waited by the door, holding Ignat's war hammer with both hands. Ignat swiped it from the young man's hand and swung it. The familiar weight settled into his palm.

The apprentice pulled the door open. Cold air washed over Ignat. He grimaced, too, and stomped through the doorway.

Outside a fresh coat of snow sheathed the ground. He didn't remember it snowing.

Okay, that was a really large wolf. Huge, in fact. The size of a horse. The adolescent boy on his back looked much less impressive though. About fifteen or so. Thin.

Big wolf or no, he had yet to meet an animal that could take a blow from his hammer.

Ignat glowered. "What is it?"

The boy stared at him. His eyes were a very odd shade, a strange green-blue.

"You are Ignat, Svarog's volhv?"

Arrogant punk. "The name is Ignat Trofimovich Kazarin. And yes, I am. Who is asking?"

"Winter sends her kind regards."

The boy opened his mouth. Magic swirled around him like a blizzard unleashed.

Ignat grabbed the apprentice volhv and yanked him down with him, flat into the snow.

A horrible wail sliced through the air, filled with despair and pain, woven of betrayal, fear, and hurt, the sound of a divine child abandoned, abused, and hopeless. It gripped Ignat's heart into its magical fist and squeezed until tears ran from his eyes. His pride snapped; his arrogance melted. Hot, despondent anguish filled him until nothing else mattered except finding the source of the pain and cradling it, trying to shelter it from all threats and sorrows.

He barely noticed the sound of breaking glass.

The wail ended. Ignat raised his head and wiped the snow from his eyes and beard. The wolf and the boy were gone.

Slowly, shakily, Svarog's volhv got up to his feet. The beautiful stained glass windows lay in shards on the snow, shattered into a thousand pieces.

Next to him, the apprentice volhv turned and sat on his butt in the snow, weeping.

"Wipe the tears, Phillip," Ignat told him.

Phillip rubbed his face with his sleeve. "What do we do now?"

"Now you'll call the glassmakers and get the windows replaced. And I'll go down to my house. It's past time my son and I had a long talk."

The End

GLOSSARY

Gods and Mythology

Ahuric Triad - In Zoroastrianism, a trinity comprised of the deities Ahura Mazda, Mithra, and Apam Napat

Anchutka - A small winged imp, not really malevolent as such, mostly cowardly. Similar to lesser fae, don't like salt or iron, keep to themselves. They only get agitated when people encroach on their territory, and even then, all they do is try to scare you with eerie noises and stare at you from the darkness

Asha - In Zoroastrianism, the force of good and truth that comes from Ahura Mazda

Auka - A small spirit of the forest, also not exactly evil; Russian-hamster-looking mouse the size of a possum with tan fur, tiny antlers, and a skunk's fluffy tan tail

Belobog - God of Light and Creation, he is the antithesis and balance to his twin brother, Chernobog

Chernobog (Chernoboshe) - God of Destruction, Darkness, and Death, the Black Flame, the Final Cold, the End of Everything, Lord of Bones, Lord of Nav. Antithesis and balance to Belobog, his brother

Demeter - Greek goddess of the harvest and agriculture

Druj - In Zoroastrianism, the force of evil and falsehood that originates from Angra Mainyu, better known as Ahriman

Ishtar - Mesopotamian goddess of love, war and fertility

Koldun - sorcerer

Koliada - Slavic Winter Solstice period and rituals

Kolovershi (Kolovertishi) - They are mischievous creatures that help a witch or wizard. Each pack of kolovershi is supposed to be slightly different based on whom they serve. Roman's look Furby-like: ranging in size from a cardinal to a barn owl, furry, with long ears that stand straight up, scaly limbs, and dexterous paws armed with small but sharp talons

Korgorusha - Resembles a black cat with an abnormally long, prehensile tail and huge sharp claws. They trail smoke as they move and can keep you sleeping under its effects

Lihoradka - Slavic mythology spirit of fever and illness. She takes possession of a body and makes them sick and contagious

Magav - Zoroastrian magus, a warrior-mage devoted to the protection of good. Farhang, the cursed new friend of Roman, is one of them

Makosh - the goddess of Fate in Slavic mythology, also a Mother Goddess figure that watches over women and childbirth. Spinning, weaving, and sheep-shearing also come under her protection

Melalo - a Romani demon creature, looks like a bird with two heads, one of them dead. Its origin story is best left unexplored

Mithra - In Zoroastrianism, the god of covenants

Mobed - Zoroastrian priest

Morena- Goddess of Winter and Death, resides in her terem in the middle of the White Cathedral in Nav. The wife and consort of Chernobog

Nav - part of the Tri-World, Nav is where the dark gods live, deities that humans fear, like Chernobog and Morena. They are not evil in the traditional sense of the world but are approached with fear by humans, as their role is to provide balance to life and light. Beyond Nav is the Chaos, and one of Chernobog's roles is to keep it from invading the Tri-World

Nechist - Small nasties, traditionally seen as evil or at least a nuisance. Little critters that range from annoying to sinister. A catch-all term for Roman's army of stray creatures, kolovershi, anchutka, auka, melalo, and whatever Roro is

Obryad - Ritual, ceremony in Slavic pagan tradition. Morena's drowning rite at the beginning of each spring is an example

Odin - Allfather, one of the main gods of Norse Mythology, god of wisdom, battle, knowledge, runic alphabet and other aspects, who rules over Valhalla and other Norse gods

Prav - Part of the Tri-World concept, Prav is the world of the gods that humans find beneficial, where the light gods—deities like Svarog the Smith, god of fire, and Belobog, god of Light and Creation—live

Striga - Slavic female demon

Svarog - Sky Father, Sky Smith, God Crafter, Father of Gods

Tri-World - The cosmic structure of the universe in Slavic paganism. It is comprised of Prav (world of the light gods), Yav (world of humans), and Nav (world of the dark gods)

Troyan - A healer god, who is part of the Nav gods. Disease and sickness are cruel and unforgiving, so humans perceive him as evil because, sometimes, no matter how much you pray to him, he doesn't answer

Vasylisa Prekrasnaya - Vasylisa the Beautiful, enchanting, alluring, and irresistible, relying on magical charm and manipulation to make armies kneel and entice powerful people to do her bidding

Vasylisa Premudraya - Vasylisa the Wise, a creature of deep magic, a sorceress with offensive powers, unpredictable and sharp

Yav - Part of the Tri-World concept, Yav is the world of humans

Void Dragon (Skiper-Zmei) - A creature of pure evil that threatens all existence

Foreign Terms Glossary

Burlak - A barge-puller from Russia's old past, a human beast of burden dragging the trade ships up the river

Imenem Chernoboga - "In the name of Chernobog." The official incantation dedicating the priest's actions to their deity

Kapisheh - Slavic Pagan temple, a place of worship

Klyuv - Beak, the name of Roman's bird-headed staff

Kumir - A carved idol or representation of a pagan god used as an object of worship

Medovuha - Slavic honey-based alcoholic beverage

Otsebyachenna - made-up nonsense

Paska - traditional enriched bread or cake made for Easter celebrations in Eastern Europe

Paskudnik- "Rascal, nasty one"

Pirogi- Slavic dumplings made of unleavened dough with various fillings, both sweet and savory

Pogibi (verb)- "Perish"

Sbiten - A honey-based winter beverage that has been consumed in Eastern Europe since the twelfth century, before the arrival of tea ("сбитень, sbit"—"to put together" in Old Russian). It usually contains honey, jam, water, and various spices or herbs

Svoloch (singular), svolochi (plural)- "Bastard"

Volhv- Pagan priest serving one of the Slavic gods or goddesses

Zaraza- Literally "infection" or "contagion," colloquially used as a slang word meaning *scumbag* or *bastard*, someone who is a creating a problem and is persistent about it.

Znak (Znek Znuck) - A sigil or sign. Chernobog's sigil can be seen on the cover of Sanctuary

ON VASYLISA AND BABA YAGA

By Rossana Sasso
This essay first appeared on Ilona Andrews' Blog
(https://ilona-andrews.com/blog/)

We are all storytellers. Stories allow us to examine what it means to be human.

Back when reading and writing were skills only a few possessed, tales were shared by word of mouth. With each oral retelling, narratives would mutate, until they became the product of a collective mind, the heritage of a particular corner of the world. Stories tell us where we come from, who we are, and how to choose the path to success. They teach us that sacrifice and sorrow, fear and obstacles are inherent and genuine parts of the human experience. They root inside our spirit and cultures and become myths and archetypes.

In Eastern European "wonder tales" (*skazka*), there is a distinct bond between nature, the humans who populate it and the magic that infuses it—including magical transformations and magical animals. It's something we are very familiar with, because we have been reading books by Ilona Andrews.

The world of Kate Daniels is a place where magic allows myth to take over, and belief literally materializes the archetypal roles as guides for certain patterns in the life of the community. Someone needs to be the Black Volhv or the Nightingale Bandit, Evdokia fulfills her Baba Yaga duties in style, and a woman takes the mantle of Vasylisa as soon as the previous one dies. It is the responsibility of chosen individuals in the community to become syncretic with these stock characters and intercede between the gods and the people whose faith sustains them.

I will paste here the usual disclaimer House Andrews provides:

"We are taking liberties with Slavic mythology in the name of artistic license, so our stories are not academic papers and shouldn't be used as such. Unfortunately, due to the absence of written records, most of what we know about Slavic mythology comes to us via oral traditions."

What is a stock character?

A stock character is a type of character audiences recognize across many narratives as part of a storytelling convention. When I say "Prince Charming," you immediately understand what I mean, even though I haven't specified whether it's Cinderella's Prince Charming or the Charming in *Shrek*. They're not the same person, clearly, yet they symbolically refer to the same role and features, which are often so stereotyped they take on caricatural proportions.

It's used as a shorthand in fairy tales to get the audience (often children) to recognize immediately who just appeared on the scene, without much work devoted to characterization. Because ain't nobody got time for that, we're trying to put the little dushegubs to sleep. *"It's the wicked witch who lives in the forest, we know her, danger ahead! Now close your eyes."*

Baba Yaga

She is often depicted as a frightening, ugly old woman who wants to eat people, flying around in a mortar with a pestle. (Evdokia was not available for comment on this particular interpretation).

She has celestial knowledge of the three horsemen—Day, Sun, and Night—indicating that she has magic and power over both night and day. Her servants are skeletal or even disembodied hands that take the sorted grain from Vasylisa the Beautiful as soon as she finishes her task. Yaga's house sits on chicken legs and is surrounded by pillars or stakes topped with skulls, and as the hero approaches, the one pillar without a skull cries, "HEAD HEAD HEAD" in an ominous voice, letting us know what awaits those who don't pass Yaga's trials.

As her son, Roman has picked up on a few of these accessories, although Chernobog, God of Bones, probably made the acquisition easier. (*Every Friday is Black Friday in Nav! Everything must go! Free giant scorpion with each purchase of bone hands! *The gods of Nav claim no responsibility for digestive issues of giant scorpion once taken off the premises.*)

Vladimir Propp (if you like Campbell's *Hero with a Thousand Faces*, definitely look into Propp's analysis of the functions of folk tales) tells us that Baba Yaga is associated not only with death and decay, but also with ancient social life, including the secret rites of initiation taking place in the forest, which is why she doesn't have the same evil-witch characteristics in all depictions.

Sometimes, she's simply a powerful guardian or shows up as an aiding figure who helps the heroine out of compassion. In Romanian stories, she is the Mother of the Forest, and the maiden's task is to take care of all her "children." Suddenly, the yard is filled with creatures, one more slithery and creepy than another—just like a certain Black Volhv's nechist pets. When the girl shows no fear, washes and lovingly tends to every single monster, she proves her kind spirit.

The one common feature of Baba Yaga's portrayals points to her connections with pre-Christian goddesses and rites of passage; even when she interacts with Vasylisa the Beautiful, this crone archetype never cares about her beauty. She cares about the initiation, the task being performed and the virtue that is manifested through it. Once Vasylisa leaves Yaga's forest with her rewards, her social status will be transformed from downtrodden peasant to wealthy woman or wife of a king. The Road of Trials the crone sets up for the maiden tests her suitability for leadership: is she hard-working and patient enough to sort through problems; is she kind enough to care about the issues of others, even when they look unpleasant; is she humble enough to ask for help or delegate?

Yaga as a mentor who changes Vasylisa's fate is an aspect inferred in the illustration "*Vasylisa at Yaga's Hut*" (1900) by Ivan Yakovlevich Bilibin. A member of the Mir Iskusstva movement that appeared in Russia at the turn of the twentieth century, Bilibin created the most famous illustrations of the archetypes present in Slavic fairy tales. He depicts the witch's hut as a warmly lit and traditionally decorated home holding the maiden's sleeve, preventing her from getting lost in the wilderness of thin and uncertain borders. Yaga's inferred role is to protect Vasylisa against destructive forces, just like the often-maligned gods that live in Nav. She stands at the balance between life and death, as she is portrayed in Kate's world, an aspect of the Triple Goddess.

The forest is a model of the Eastern European world, the Tri-World, as opposed to signifying the uncivilized and taboo unknown inhabited by barbarians, as it often does in Western European myth. It is a liminal and dangerous space filled with supernatural forces, but at the same time, it is understood as native to the people who created these stories. They build homes at the forest's edge and they travel inside it seeking sustenance and magical help.

Vasylisa

Vasylisa is the stock fairy tale princess character. She also has several interpretations, with one thing in common: in all of her appearances, she is strong.

Less the princess who waits to be rescued, Vasylisa is part of the female archetypes in Slavic fairy tales that Get Stuff Done: like Yaga, Koshechka-Havroshechka, or Marya Morevna, who is basically a female bogatyr (a Queen Knight who leads armies in war and has previously defeated that most villainous of wizard stock characters—Koschei the Deathless).

The stories she appears in can be found in Alexander Afanasyev's collection of Russian Fairy Tales: *Vasylisa the Beautiful*; *The Firebird and Princess Vasylisa*; *The Frog Tsarevna*; *The Sea Tsar and Vasylisa the Wise*, and *Vasylisa the Priest's Daughter*.

Her two main aspects are Vasylisa Prekrasnaya (Прекрасная) and Premudraya (Премудрая): the Beautiful and the Wise. Technically, the prefix "pre" is there to elevate whatever comes after it to a superior state (in our case *krasiva*—beautiful and *mudraya*—wise), so her titles are Overly Beautiful and Very Wise, in the sense of almost too much. Main character energy, Vasylisa has it.

We've seen how Vasylisa the Beautiful improves her lot in life through her virtues. Vasylisa the Wise's journey, by contrast, demonstrates great powers and magical knowledge—she fights, conjures, and transmutes the elements and herself. She's clearly part of the same witch and wizard group as Koschei, Yaga, and the Sea Tsar—and she's adept at sorcery and tipping the scales of destiny.

When Prince Ivan (as the Fool he is) burns Vasylisa the Wise's frog skin in the *Frog Tsarevna*, he delays the breaking of the curse that holds her captive. Baba Yaga is the one who puts him through trials, and only when he proves worthy can he get access to Vasylisa again. She is supremely not bothered and greets him with, "Oh, you have been a long time coming, Prince Ivan! I almost married someone else." A certain Horde I know (and ship alongside to) would say poor Ivan is really out of his league and

His Sexiness the Black Volhv is much more Vasylisa the Wise's speed.

In the *Sea Tsar* story, she plays the part of Ariadne. Vasylisa's magic interventions are the only reason her betrothed is able to survive the tasks her father sets out for him. Like Ariadne, she is forgotten by the prince who moves on once they marry. The Wise doesn't wait for gods or heroes in the manner of her Greek counterpart, however. She marches to his castle and claims her man back, in the middle of his wedding to someone else. It was the fuck around times, it was the find out times.

Even when she's initially Not-Too-Wise, like in *The Firebird and Vasylisa Tsarevna*, where she gets tempted by greed enough to be kidnapped, she uses her power to take charge of her own destiny in ways fairy tale princesses rarely do. The hunter who has proven himself through all the trials is the husband Vasylisa desires, not the king who is only attempting to get credit for another's success. The last courtship challenge she sets is for the two men to bathe in the milk of her magical mares. One emerges transformed, healed and handsome. The other is boiled to death. Vasylisa the Powerful made her choice.

Do not mess with Vasylisa!

Bibliography:

Jack V. Haney (Ed), (2015). *The Complete Folktales of A. N. Afanas'ev, Volumes I and II*. University Press of Mississippi.

Vladimir Yakolevich Propp, (2012). *The Russian Folktale*. Wayne State University Press.

Kolesnik, M.A. *et al.* (2017). *Analysis of the Illustrations by Ivan Yakovlevich Bilbin (1876-1942) to Russian fairy, SGEM International Multidisciplinary Scientific Conferences on Social Sciences and Arts*, Available at https://www.academia.edu/ (Accessed on April 17 2024).

ALSO BY ILONA ANDREWS

Roman's Chronicles

SANCTUARY

Kate Daniels: Wilmington Years

MAGIC TIDES

MAGIC CLAIMS

Kate Daniels World

BLOOD HEIR

Kate Daniels Series

MAGIC BITES

MAGIC BLEEDS

MAGIC BURNS

MAGIC STRIKES

MAGIC MOURNS

MAGIC BLEEDS

MAGIC DREAMS

MAGIC SLAYS

GUNMETAL MAGIC

MAGIC GIFTS

MAGIC RISES

MAGIC BREAKS

MAGIC STEALS

MAGIC SHIFTS

MAGIC STARS

MAGIC BINDS

MAGIC TRIUMPHS

The Iron Covenant

IRON AND MAGIC

UNTITLED IRON AND MAGIC #2

Hidden Legacy Series

BURN FOR ME

WHITE HOT

WILDFIRE

DIAMOND FIRE

SAPPHIRE FLAMES

EMERALD BLAZE

RUBY FEVER

Innkeeper Chronicles Series

CLEAN SWEEP

SWEEP IN PEACE

ONE FELL SWEEP

SWEEP OF THE BLADE

SWEEP WITH ME

SWEEP OF THE HEART

Kinsmen

SILENT BLADE

SILVER SHARK

THE KINSMEN UNIVERSE (anthology with both SILENT BLADE and SILVER SHARK)

FATED BLADES

ABOUT THE AUTHOR

Ilona Andrews is the pseudonym for a husband-and-wife writing team, Gordon and Ilona. They currently reside in Texas with their two children and numerous dogs and cats. The couple are the #1 *New York Times* and *USA Today* bestselling authors of the Kate Daniels and Kate Daniels World novels as well as The Edge and Hidden Legacy series. They also write the Innkeeper Chronicles series, which they post as a free weekly serial.

For a complete list of their books, fun extras, and Innkeeper installments, please visit their website www.ilona-andrews.com .

Printed in the USA
CPSIA information can be obtained
at www.ICGtesting.com
LVHW010354291024
795002LV00001B/238